DRAGON WARRIORS
THE ULTIMATE ROLE-PLAYING GAME

DRAGON WARRIORS is the key to a magic world. A land of cobwebbed forests and haunted castles. A land where dire monsters lurk in the shadows of the night, where hobgoblins shriek across the bleak and misty moors, where wizards and armoured warriors roam dank dungeons in their quest for gold and glory. The realm of your imagination.

THE WAY OF WIZARDRY is the second title in the DRAGON WARRIORS series and expands the game to include the magical arts. Take on the mantle of a Mystic or a spell-casting Sorcerer: more than a hundred spells, potions and arcane magical devices await within for you and your friends, together with two eerie scenarios to test your nerve and magical skills!

The authors, Dave Morris and Oliver Johnson, first met at Oxford University through a mutual interest in role-playing games. Since then they have worked on a free-lance basis – devising, developing and writing numerous solo fantasy gamebooks and contributing to specialist fantasy magazines.

Dave Morris now works full-time as a writer; Oliver Johnson works as an Editor with Corgi Books.

D1665625

DRAGON WARRIORS

All published by Corgi Books

THE ULTIMATE ROLE-PLAYING GAME

DRAGON WARRIORS

BOOK TWO

The Way of Wizardry

by Dave Morris

**Illustrated by Leo Hartas,
Jeremy Ford and Bob Harvey**

CORGI BOOKS
A DIVISION OF TRANSWORLD PUBLISHERS LTD.

DRAGON WARRIORS BOOK TWO: THE WAY OF WIZARDRY

A CORGI BOOK 0 552 522880

First published in Great Britain by Corgi Books

PRINTING HISTORY
Corgi edition published 1985

Text copyright © Dave Morris 1985
Illustrations copyright © Transworld Publishers Ltd. 1985

Corgi Books are published by
Transworld Publishers Ltd., Century House,
61 – 63 Uxbridge Road,
Ealing, London W5 5SA,
England

Printed and bound in Great Britain by
Cox & Wyman Ltd., Reading, Berks.

Contents

Premonition (sixth sense)
ESP (seventh sense)
Enchantment of arms & armour

Chapter Four: TREASURE

Treasure table
Monsters' treasure hoards
NPC weapons & equipment
Trading

Chapter Five: ITEMS WEIRD & WONDROUS

Enchanted armour
Enchanted weapons
Scrolls
Potions & magical compounds
Amulets & talismans
Rings
Artifacts
Relics

Chapter Six: ADVENTURE SCENARIOS

Scenario 1: "A Shadow on the Mist"
Scenario 2: "Hunter's Moon"

To Barbara

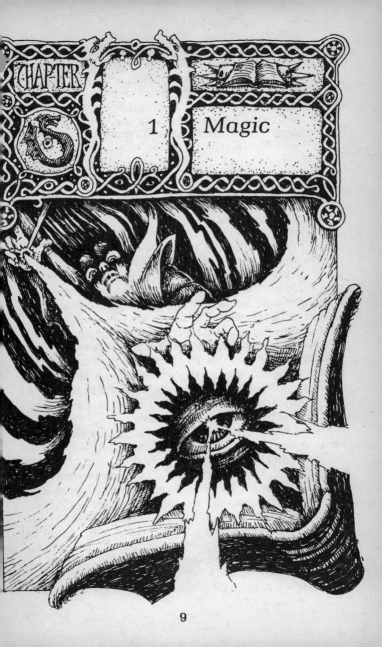

CHAPTER 1 Magic

In the DRAGON WARRIORS game there are two magic-using Professions. *Sorcerers* are those who seek to master the arcane enchantments which enable them to draw energy from other dimensions and channel it according to their wishes. They make poor fighters, but their spells can be quite devastating. *Mystics*, on the other hand, meditate so as to harmonize themselves with the unseen forces of Nature – perhaps we would call them 'psionics' in modern terminology. Mystics learn something of the fighting arts, and many of their spells serve to enhance the Mystic's own physical and mental prowess.

Any player choosing to be a Sorcerer or a Mystic will soon realize the big difference between the magic-using Professions and the fighting Professions. Sorcerers and Mystics are able to use a lot of power in a short time, but once their spells are exhausted they are relatively weak. A Sorcerer or Mystic who comes, fresh and with spells undiminished, to a battle with a Knight or Barbarian of similar rank will usually win. If the Sorcerer/Mystic had already used his day's spells, however, the reverse would be true. Over a typical adventure – four hours (game-time) in a monster-ridden dungeon, say – the whole thing averages out. As a GamesMaster, you may find it useful to remember that short adventures favour the magic-users while long adventures favour the fighters.

There is one group of spells usable by Sorcerers, another usable by Mystics. The two groups are quite different, but that is not the only distinction between Sorcerers and Mystics. When a Sorcerer casts a spell, he expends *Magic Points* to do so; when he has used up all his *Magic Points*, he can use no more spells that day. Mystics do not have *Magic Points*. When a Mystic casts a spell, he makes a check to see whether he 'fatigues' his spellcasting ability; when this psionic 'fatigue' occurs, the Mystic can cast no more spells that day. On average, a Mystic and a Sorcerer of equal rank will be able to use roughly the same number of spells in a day

– but, whereas the Sorcerer always knows precisely how much spell-power (in the form of *Magic Points*) he has left, the Mystic can never be sure when he is going to suffer 'fatigue'. Mystics have to get used to a life of uncertainty.

Magical Combat Factors (revisited)

Chapter Two of the first DRAGON WARRIORS book briefly mentioned that Sorcerers and Mystics have a MAGICAL ATTACK score. The basic MAGICAL ATTACK score is 15 in the case of Sorcerers and 14 in the case of Mystics. This basic score is modified if the character's *Intelligence* and/or *Psychic Talent* are outside the average range:

	Characteristic score															
	3	4	5	6	7	8	9	10	11	12	13	14	15	16	17	18
Intelligence	– 1 MAGICAL ATTACK													+ 1 MAGICAL ATTACK		
Psychic Talent	(Characters with Psychic Talent 8 or less cannot use magic.)										+ 1 MAGICAL ATTACK			+ 2 MAGICAL ATTACK		

Spells

Sorcerer spells and Mystic spells have some features in common. The following points are the same for both groups.

How long does the spell last?

Some spells last only a few seconds. If you blinked, you might miss a *Shadowbolt* or a *Dragonbreath* altogether. Effectively, such spells are instantaneous.

Spells which continue to operate for more than one Combat Round are called *durational*. A glance through

11

the spell lists of Chapters Two and Three will show that all durational spells are indicated as such. In some cases a specific duration is given (eg 'Moonglow – lasts for ten minutes'). Where it is not, there is only the mysterious statement: 'Spell Expiry Roll applies'. What does this entail?

A Spell Expiry Roll is made by rolling two six-sided dice (2d6). On a roll of 2 – 11, the spell continues to operate. On a roll of 12, it wears off. This Spell Expiry Roll is made at the start of each Combat Round following that in which the spell was cast. (If a Sorcerer/Mystic has several spells going at one time, he must make a separate Spell Expiry Roll for each. So a duel between two high-ranking characters can involve a whole series of 2d6 rolls at the beginning of each new Round, as the duellists check for each of their protective enchantments in turn.)

How does the spell affect its victim?

Every attack spell falls into one of two categories. 'Direct-attack' spells are those which have a direct supernatural effect on the victim – turn him to stone, hypnotise him, etc. 'Indirect-attack' spells are those which create some secondary effect such as a jet of flame or a bolt of lightning.

Looking through the description of the *Dragon-breath* spell, you may not think there is anything particularly indirect about it. It *is* indirect-attack, though, because the way in which it harms its victim is *physical, not supernatural*. The spell creates a jet of fire. If the intended victim is not quick on his feet and/or well-armoured, he will get burned. His intrinsic resistance to magic (ie MAGICAL DEFENCE) is irrelevant.

In practice, direct-attack spells are those which require the caster to match his own MAGICAL ATTACK against his intended target's MAGICAL

DEFENCE. Indirect-attack spells require the caster to match the spell's intrinsic SPEED against the victim's EVASION.

EXAMPLE

Two 1st rank Sorcerers, Gothique and Kaos, are squaring off for a duel. Gothique acts first and, since he knows his opponent has below average *Reflexes*, opens with *Dragonbreath*. The spell's SPEED is 12 and Kaos's EVASION score is only 2, so Gothique needs to roll 10 or less on 2d10 for the flame to hit. He rolls a '5' and then rolls 1d6 + 6 to determine how much damage Kaos takes.

Scorched but still standing, Kaos prepares to retaliate. He can see that his foe is wearing armour which, even though it is only hardened leather, would give him some protection against *Dragonbreath*. He therefore throws a *Weaken* spell. Kaos has a MAGICAL ATTACK score of 17 (he's very highly psychic). Matched against Gothique's MAGICAL DEFENCE of 5, this means that Kaos has to roll 12 or less on 2d10 for the spell to take effect. He rolls a '9', Gothique succumbs to the *Weaken* spell, and a new Combat Round begins.

How far can the spell reach?

Where relevant, a maximum range is given for each spell. When Sorcerers and Mystics are in an adventuring party it becomes particularly important to have some way of keeping track of where each character is standing (such as marked counters or figurines). Otherwise there will be numerous exhausting arguments along the lines of 'I'm sure that Orc is in range for a *Shadowbolt*' or 'He can't have hit me with *Fossilize* – I'm too far away!' Figurines make the whole combat situation clear, eliminating any need for dispute.

Can spells be overlapped?

Two different spells can. In fact, it is theoretically possible to have any number of different durational spells going at one time. A Sorcerer who's feeling really nasty (or cautious) might put on *Spell Screen*, *Vorpal Blade*, *Warding*, *Invisibility* and *Armour* (and maybe a few others as well) before wading into a fight.

The same spell cannot, however, be 'doubled up' to get twice the benefit. A Sorcerer who casts *Vorpal Blade* twice has simply wasted 7 *Magic Points* – he doesn't get two swords to fight with!

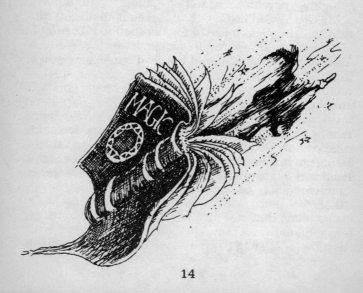

CHAPTER 5 / 2 / Sorcerers

Minimum Requirements

A player who wishes his character to be a Sorcerer must roll scores of at least 9 for both *Intelligence* and *Psychic Talent*. If these scores are below average, the character is not qualified to study sorcery.

Casting Spells

The spells are divided into levels of increasing power and complexity. A Sorcerer cannot cast a spell of higher level than his rank. Spells cost *Magic Points* to cast – 1 *MP* for a first level spell, 2 *MP* for a second level, etc. When a Sorcerer casts a spell, he deducts the appropriate number of *Magic Points* from his *Magic Point* score. When this score reaches 0, the Sorcerer can cast no more spells that day. The *Magic Point* score increases with rank (of course!), as shown in the following table.

Magic Points

Sorcerer's rank	Magic Points usable/day
1st	4
2nd	8
3rd	12
4th	15
5th	19
6th	23
7th	25
8th	28
9th	31
10th	35

(and + 4 *MPs* per rank thereafter)

Expended *Magic Points* regenerate at precisely midnight.

EXAMPLE

Lyona is a 2nd rank Sorceress, and thus has a normal (undepleted) *Magic Point* score of 8. During one adventure, she casts a *Tangleroots*, a *Weaken* and two *Dragonbreath* spells, leaving her with 3 *Magic Points*. She manages to avoid any further trouble that day, and at midnight her *Magic Point* total is restored to its normal score of 8.

Using Extra Magic Points

A Sorcerer may choose to put additional *Magic Points* into a spell, above the basic *MP* cost of the spell. There is no advantage to be gained doing this with an indirect-attack spell – it is a tactic to be used with direct-attack spells, to give them more chance of getting through an enemy's magical barriers. If a Sorcerer suspects his opponent has a *Wall of Magic* operating, putting an extra few *Magic Points* into the

Dishearten spell he's casting may seem a worthwhile investment.

Sorcerers and Armour

There is nothing to stop a Sorcerer wearing heavy armour, but it is not usually a good idea. Sorcerers are not trained to fight in armour, for one thing, and suffer combat penalties if they do so (see Chapter Three of DRAGON WARRIORS 1). More seriously, armour hampers the freedom of movement necessary if the Sorcerer is to make accurate occult gestures. Certain types of armour give a chance of miscasting any spell, as follows.

Armour worn	Chance of miscast spell
Ringmail	10%
Chainmail	20%
Plate	30%

This applies to each spell the Sorcerer casts. For instance, Limorien, a Sorcerer who insists on wearing plate armour, has a 30% chance of miscasting any spell. Every time he attempts a spell, he must roll d100. On a roll of 01 – 30, he has miscast it.

A Sorcerer miscasting a spell must pay twice the normal *Magic Point* cost of the spell. Instead of getting the spell he wanted, he rolls randomly among all the spells of the same level. If Limorien attempts a *Warding* and miscasts it, he has to roll a six-sided die. Say he rolls a '5' – this means he actually casts, not *Warding*, but the fifth spell of level two: *Tangleroots*. Poor Limorien not only pays the exorbitant cost of 4 *Magic Points*, but he has to dodge his own *Tangleroots* spell!

Terminating a Spell

A Sorcerer can cancel his own durational spells at any time. He does not need to wait for the spell to wear off.

This is a definite action – he has to 'will' the spell to terminate – and takes one Combat Round.

When a Sorcerer terminates a durational spell to which a Spell Expiry Roll applies, he gets back half the *Magic Points* (rounded down) that he expended to cast it.

EXAMPLE

Lyona is on a dungeon adventure with some friends. Their first encounter is with some Skeletons. These are defeated after a short skirmish, during which Lyona has cast *Moonglow, Hold Off The Dead* and *Tangleroots*. She has 3 *Magic Points* left.

Since the Skeleton she caught with *Tangleroots* has now been slain by one of her comrades, Lyona terminates the spell. Her *Magic Points* score is back up to 4.

She is about to terminate the *Hold Off The Dead* spell and get an *MP* back for that as well, but before she gets the chance its Spell Expiry Roll comes up '12' and it wears off naturally.

Cancelling the *Moonglow* would not give her back any MPs. *Moonglow* is one of the handful of durational spells which do not take a Spell Expiry Roll. (Even if it did, she would get no points for cancelling it. Can you see why?)

CHARACTER CREATION SUMMARY – Sorcerers

A. *Strength, Reflexes, Intelligence, Psychic Talent* and *Looks*: roll 3d6 for each
    (*Intelligence* and *Psychic Talent* must both be at least 9)

B. *Health Points*: roll 1d6 + 4

C. Basic ATTACK 11, DEFENCE 5

D. Basic MAGICAL ATTACK 15, MAGICAL DEFENCE 5

E.   Basic EVASION 3

F.   Initially equipped with lantern, flint-&-tinder, backpack, dagger, shortsword or staff, 20 Florins, any two potions from the following: Dexterity, Occult Acuity, Strength, Healing and Replenishment. (The potions are a gift from the Master Sorcerer under whom the character served his apprenticeship. This is a long-established tradition.)

G.   *Magic Points*: 4

This summary indicates how the Character Sheet should be filled out for a 1st rank Sorcerer (with appropriate modifications for *Strength, Intelligence*, etc).

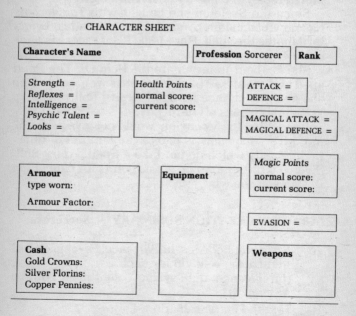

CHARACTER SHEET

| Character's Name | Profession Sorcerer | Rank |

Strength =
Reflexes =
Intelligence =
Psychic Talent =
Looks =

Health Points
normal score:
current score:

ATTACK =
DEFENCE =

MAGICAL ATTACK =
MAGICAL DEFENCE =

Armour
type worn:

Armour Factor:

Equipment

Magic Points
normal score:
current score:

EVASION =

Cash
Gold Crowns:
Silver Florins:
Copper Pennies:

Weapons

Each player will require a blank Character Sheet. Permission is granted to make photocopies. A full sized Character Sheet will be found at the back of the book.

The Spells

The list below shows all the spells usable by Sorcerers. The two important points to remember are, firstly, that a spell's level is also the number of *Magic Points* needed to cast it and, secondly, a Sorcerer can cast only those spells whose level does not exceed his rank.

Spells of Level One
  DRAGONBREATH
  IMAGE
  LESSER HEALING
  MOONGLOW
  PORTAL
  WEAKEN

Spells of Level Two
  DETECT AURA
  HOLD OFF THE DEAD
  INFLICT WOUND
  PEER
  TANGLEROOTS
  WARDING

Spells of Level Three
  BANQUET
  BEACON
  COMMAND
  GREATER HEALING
  ILLUSION
  WOLFCALL

Spells of Level Four
  ANTIDOTE
  CURSE
  DISEASE
  ORACLE
  SHADOWBOLT
  WALL OF MAGIC

Spells of Level Five
  BANISH
  DIVINATION
  FOSSILIZE
  MANTLET
  REANIMATE THE
    DEAD
  TRANSFIX

Spells of Level Six
  ARMOUR
  CURE DISEASE
  DISHEARTEN
  DISPEL MAGIC
  PHANTASM
  SWORD OF
    DAMOCLES

Spells of Level Seven
  DEATHLIGHT
  ENSLAVE
  NOVA
  SPELL SCREEN
  STASIS
  VORPAL BLADE

Spells of Level Eight
  ASTRAL GATE
  BASTION
  BURDEN
  DESTRIER
  EVIL EYE
  RUNE

21

Spells of Level Nine
ANIMATE BONES
BATTLEMASTER
FIRESTORM
INVISIBILITY
MIRACLE CURE
RAISE FOG

Spells of Level Ten
DOPPELGANGER
HECATOMB
PENTACLE OF
ENTRAPMENT
RESURRECT
SCRY
TRANSFORMATION

Spells of Level One

DRAGONBREATH

Match spell's SPEED of 12 vs target's EVASION
Range: 20m

This spell creates a narrow jet of flame which can be directed at a single target. If the target fails to dodge the flame he takes 1d6 + 6 *Health Points* damage. This damage roll is reduced by the target's Armour Factor, however (so a character in plate armour would lose only 1d6 + 1 *HP*).

IMAGE

Range: 20m
Durational – (see below)

The caster can create a visual image of no greater than man-size; this is nearly perfect, and has only a 10% chance of being recognized to be an illusion. The *Image* is a kind of hologram, and cannot be made to move around. It will last until touched or *Dispelled*.

LESSER HEALING

Range: touch

This spell restores 2 *Health Points* to a wounded

character. It will not increase his *Health Point* score above its normal (unwounded) level, of course. *Lesser Healing* cannot bring a character back from the dead – such a feat is possible in the DRAGON WARRIORS world, but more potent sorcery than this is needed!

MOONGLOW

Durational – lasts for ten minutes

A circle of light 5m in radius surrounds the caster, who can dim the intensity to zero or brighten it to about the level of the full moon's light, at will. Unlike torchlight, the illumination provided by this spell is sufficiently diffuse that it may not alert monsters lurking nearby. A party of characters using no other light source but *Moonglow* have a chance (the usual 1 in 6) of surprising any monster they meet.

PORTAL

Range: touch
Durational – (see below)

This spell may be used in either of two ways. *Open Portal* will thrust open any door which could normally be forced by a character of *Strength* 16. The second mode of the spell, *Close Portal*, shuts and locks a door magically. This form of the spell is durational, and will stay in effect until *Dispelled* or broken by physical force.

WEAKEN

Match caster's MAGICAL ATTACK vs target's MAGICAL DEFENCE
Range: 20m
Durational – Spell Expiry Roll applies

The character on whom this spell takes effects will be weakened. He temporarily loses 2 ATTACK points and inflicts 1 less point of damage than usual when striking in combat.

Spells of Level Two (2 Magic Points to cast)

DETECT AURA

Durational — Spell Expiry Roll applies

This spell enables the caster (or another on whom he casts the spell) to see the supernatural aura which surrounds enchanted beings and objects.

HOLD OFF THE DEAD

Match caster's MAGICAL ATTACK vs undead's MAGICAL DEFENCE
Durational — Spell Expiry Roll applies

This spell creates a zone around the caster, 2m in radius, which affects undead whose rank-equivalent does not exceed the caster's rank. If such undead enter the zone they are immediately subject to a magical attack which, if successful, prevents them from approaching the caster as long as his spell lasts.

INFLICT WOUND

Match caster's MAGICAL ATTACK vs target's MAGICAL DEFENCE
Range: 3m

If successful, this inflicts a 5 *Health Point* wound on the victim. Armour provides no protection against this damage.

PEER

Range: 20m
Durational – Spell Expiry Roll applies (and see below)

When this spell is cast, the Sorcerer specifies any point within the spell's range (eg '14m due north', '5m straight down', etc). He is then able to see anything that is happening within 3m of the specified point as though he were standing there. The spell is not hampered by intervening walls or floors unless these are made of metal; more than 2cm thickness of metal will block a Peer spell. The spell will expire immediately if the caster moves around while it is operating.

TANGLEROOTS

Match spell's SPEED of 14 vs target's EVASION
Range: 15m
Durational – Spell Expiry Roll applies

This spell affects one target, causing a tangle of magical creepers to sprout out of the ground and ensnare his legs. If the target fails to leap clear then he is caught and immobilized. With an edged weapon it is possible to cut oneself free within 2 – 8 Combat Rounds (roll 2d4); beings of great strength (Strength 16 or more) will be able to pull free of the Tangleroots in only 1 – 3 rounds, animals such as Wolves will take 2 – 12 rounds to claw and chew through the roots. This spell is commonly used either to hold any enemy while trying to escape from him, or to prevent him evading a more devastating follow-up spell.

WARDING

Durational – Spell Expiry Roll applies

Warding enhances the Sorcerer's luck in combat. Any

character attempting a Hit Roll against him, whether in melee or with a missile weapon, must add 2 to the d20 score.

Sorcerer Spells of Level Three (3 Magic Points to cast)

BANQUET

Enough food and drink is created to provide one meal for five people. The food is nourishing but – despite the spell's appetising name – rather bland. Few would care to eat it if they had a choice; but when adventurers are starving, they will fall upon *Banquet* fare enthusiastically enough!

BEACON

Range: 15m
Durational – Spell Expiry Roll applies

If any invisible object or being is within range when *Beacon* is cast, the spell causes a glowing ball of green light to appear just above it. This light will move as the invisible object/being moves, thus marking out its location.

COMMAND

Match caster's MAGICAL ATTACK vs target's MAGICAL DEFENCE
Range: 5m
Durational: Spell Expiry Roll applies

A successful casting of this spell brings the victim (who must be of 1st – 3rd rank) under the Sorcerer's control. He will then do whatever the caster tells him to do.

Commanded beings do not become mindless slaves; they retain their normal intelligence and ability to reason, and are thus capable of following quite complex orders. Language barriers may be a problem – if the victim cannot understand what his 'master' is saying to him then he will simply act in what he believes to be his master's best interests.

GREATER HEALING

Range: 5m

A more powerful version of *Lesser Healing*. It restores 7 *Health Points* to the recipient, with the same provisos as for the level one spell.

ILLUSION

Range: 20m
Durational – Spell Expiry Roll applies

This spell creates an illusion no greater than two cubic metres in volume. This differs from an *Image* in two ways; the *Illusion* will move as the caster wishes, and it fools not just sight but the other natural senses as well. There is thus very little chance of distinguishing an Illusion from the real thing; even a rigorous examination gives only a 5% chance of this. If he wishes, the Sorcerer can cast *Illusion* over a character (himself included) in order to provide a near-perfect disguise. When overlapped in this way, the *Illusion* must be equal in at least one linear dimension to the thing it is covering. A man could thus be covered by the *Illusion* of a 2m long snake, but not by the *Illusion* of a gnat.

It is important to remember that *Illusions* exist only in the minds of those who behold them. An *Illusion* could not cast a spell, inflict a wound, carry treasure, open doors, or in any other way affect the real world.

WOLFCALL

Durational – Spell Expiry Roll applies

This spell is usable only out-of-doors – in moorland, woods and dense forest, the wild places where Wolves hunt. It summons one Wolf to the caster's side to fight for him. The Wolf will arrive 2–12 Combat Rounds after the spell is cast and will then remain until the spell wears off. The Sorcerer does not start making Spell Expiry Rolls until the Wolf turns up.

(A note for the literal-minded: there does not actually have to be a Wolf nearby for *Wolfcall* to work. The Wolf may in fact be brought across miles of countryside in barely a minute, by the working of the Sorcerer's magic.)

Sorcerer Spells of Level Four (4 Magic Points to cast)

ANTIDOTE

Range: 5m

This reduces the potency of poisons or drugs in a character's bloodstream. A poison which normally requires a 3d6 roll compared to the character's *Strength* (see Book One) is reduced to one which requires a 2d6 roll, etc. The spell must be applied within one Combat Round (six seconds) of the character being poisoned. It does not reverse any damage or other effects already caused by the poison.

CURSE

Match caster's MAGICAL ATTACK vs target's MAGICAL DEFENCE
Range: 15m
Durational – lasts until Dispelled

This spell affects up to four beings (roll 1d4), cursing them with bad luck if it is successful. Cursed beings must adjust all their die rolls by 2 so as to make them less favourable − ie, + 2 to the die score when making a Hit Roll, − 2 when making an Armour Bypass Roll, etc.

DISEASE

Match caster's MAGICAL ATTACK vs target's MAGICAL DEFENCE
Range: 15m

A single living being may be afflicted with a rotting disease. The victim loses 2 *Health Points* every Combat Round until cured or dead.

ORACLE

Durational − lasts for one minute

The Sorcerer attunes himself to the spirit world and is able to ask up to three questions. The questions must be phrased in such a way that they can be answered by a yes or a no. The spirits have a 75% chance of knowing the answer to any given question. (The Games-Master rolls d100. On 01-75 they know the answer; on rolls of 76 − 00 they don't.) If they do not know the answer to a question, or if the question is worded vaguely, the spirits will give a random answer (roll d6: 1 − 3 = yes, 4 − 6 = no), and they will then stick to that answer if asked the same question again.

The spirits can speak only of events concerning the past and present. They cannot see into the future, nor answer questions which concern a character's thoughts and motives. Thus, a Sorcerer could ask 'Have my companions ever discussed murdering me?' but not 'Have any of my companions ever thought of murdering me?'

SHADOWBOLT

Match spell's SPEED of 14 vs target's EVASION
Range: 20m

Causes an ebon bolt of energy to shoot from the
caster's hand to strike a single being. If the bolt hits, it
does 2d6 + 10 HP damage. The damage roll is reduced
by a number equal to the target's Armour Factor, if any
(cf the *Dragonbreath* spell).

WALL OF MAGIC

Durational – Spell Expiry Roll applies (and see
below)

The caster – or another on whom he casts the spell –
is surrounded by a protective zone that will block
enemy spells. The caster may expend as many points
as he likes when casting the *Wall of Magic* (down to a
minimum of 4 MP), and this is the number of *Magic
Points* the *Wall* will absorb from spells cast into it.
Once it has absorbed its *Magic Point* limit, the *Wall* collapses. *Wall of Magic* blocks only *direct-attack* spells,
however – ie, those that involve a MAGICAL ATTACK
vs MAGICAL DEFENCE roll. *Indirect-attack* spells
such as *Shadowbolt* are unaffected.

If the *Wall* collapses without having absorbed all the
Magic Points from an incoming spell, the spell still has
a chance of taking effect, but the attacking Sorcerer
(or Mystic) must adjust his attack die roll by the difference between the number of *MP*'s left in the spell
and the spell's Level. Suppose Eldrin the Crafty has put
up a 5 *MP Wall of Magic*. His arch-foe Nebulos attacks
him with a *Disease* spell, which is completely absorbed
but which knocks the *Wall* down to 1 *MP* in the process.
In the next Combat Round, Nebulos casts a *Curse*.
Eldrin's *Wall of Magic* collapses after absorbing 1 *MP*
from the *Curse*. Nebulos matches his MAGICAL
ATTACK against Eldrin's MAGICAL DEFENCE to

resolve his *Curse*, but must add 1 to the 2d10 roll because the *Curse* is of reduced strength.

Sorcerer Spells of Level Five (5 Magic Points to cast)

BANISH

> Match caster's MAGICAL ATTACK vs target's MAGICAL DEFENCE
> range: touch
> Durational – lasts until Dispelled

For this spell to take effect, the caster must actually touch his intended victim in the Combat Round following that in which he cast the spell. This means that the caster must make a successful Hit Roll on his opponent – though no Armour Bypass Roll is needed, as it is sufficient that he merely touch the opponent's clothing or armour. If the spell takes effect, the victim is banished to limbo, and can only be freed at the caster's whim or if a *Dispel Magic* is cast at the spot where the victim disappeared. A Sorcerer can communicate in his dreams with those he has banished, and will usually find them quite eager to barter information and secrets in return for a promise of freedom from limbo.

DIVINATION

> Durational – lasts one minute

A modification of the *Oracle* spell which enables the caster to ask a question even if the answer is not a simple yes/no. Only one question may be asked, and there is still the same limit (75%) on accuracy. The spirits will often answer in the form of a rhyme, riddle or obscure clue – the GM is urged to be inventive and evasive! A Sorcerer may not cast more than one *Divination* in a single day.

FOSSILIZE

Match caster's MAGICAL ATTACK vs target's
MAGICAL DEFENCE
Range: 20m
Durational – lasts until Dispelled

One being is turned to stone, along with anything he is
wearing or carrying. *Fossilize* has no effect on
Gargoyles (their bodies are made of rock in the first
place) nor, for obvious reasons, on non-corporeal creatures such as Spectres.

MANTLET

Durational – Spell Expiry Roll applies

This highly useful spell surrounds the caster with an
enchanted zone 3m in radius. Any arrow, quarrel,
slingshot or other missile entering this zone will fall
harmlessly to the ground. Magical or extremely large
(more than 20kg) projectiles are not impeded by the
spell, however.

REANIMATE THE DEAD

Range: 5m
Durational – Spell Expiry Roll applies

By means of this necromantic spell, the Sorcerer can
raise up to six (roll 1d6) dead Humans, Elves or
Dwarves as Zombies (see Book One) under his control.
Zombies, having only limited intelligence, will not be
able to comprehend complex instructions – the
Sorcerer must limit his commands to four words or
less.

TRANSFIX

Match caster's MAGICAL ATTACK vs targets'
MAGICAL DEFENCE
Range: 20m
Durational – Spell Expiry Roll applies (and see
below)

2 – 8 beings (roll 2d4 for the number affected) suffer a
'brainstorm' which causes them to stop what they are
doing and stand passively until the spell wears off.
Afterwards, they will be unable to remember anything
that happened while the spell was in effect or in the
two Combat Rounds just before it was cast. If a *Trans-
fixed* character is attacked, the spell is immediately
broken.

Sorcerer Spells of Level Six (6 Magic Points to cast)

ARMOUR

Durational – Spell Expiry Roll applies

The caster of the spell becomes engirded in jet black
plate armour. This provides an Armour Factor of 6
and, unlike normal armour, does not hamper the Sorcerer's spellcasting ability. Any clothing or armour the
caster is already wearing is transformed for the duration of the spell – one cannot cast it on top of a suit of
normal plate and then claim an AF of 11!

CURE DISEASE

Range: 1m

The beneficiary of this valued spell is cleansed of all ill-
nesses, whether natural or uncanny in origin. Damage
already suffered as a result of the disease is not
healed, however.

DISHEARTEN

Match caster's MAGICAL ATTACK vs target's
MAGICAL DEFENCE
Range: 30m

A far more terrible spell than its euphemistic name
suggests – this causes the victim's heart to explode,
killing him instantly. Naturally, it has no effect
on Undead or on creatures such as Gargoyles,
Death's-Heads, etc, which have no heart. A useful side-
effect of the spell is that even if it fails to take effect,
the target still loses 1d4 *HP* as though from a painful
kick to the unprotected chest.

DISPEL MAGIC

Range: 5m

When the *Dispel Magic* is cast, any durational spells
operating within its range (except for those which cost
more *Magic Points* than are used in the *Dispel Magic*)
immediately expire. *Dispel Magic* is not directional,
and may therefore terminate the caster's own durational spells as well as those of his enemies.

PHANTASM

Durational – Spell Expiry Roll applies

The Sorcerer draws ectoplasm from another dimension and is able to fashion it into a creature to do his
bidding. The creature may be whatever the Sorcerer
wishes, as long as it is no larger than about twice man-
size. Regardless of its outward appearance, the
Phantasm's abilities and characteristics are always
the same: MAGICAL DEFENCE of 8, EVASION of 5,
Armour Factor 4, 4–24 *Health Points* (roll 4d6).
ATTACK and DEFENCE must sum to 28, but may be
chosen by the caster within this limitation. When

Phantasms strike in combat they always use d10 for Armour Bypass Rolls and inflict 5 *HP* on a successful hit. The Phantasm's movement rate corresponds to that of the creature it resembles – 10m/Combat Round if Human, etc.

SWORD OF DAMOCLES

Range: 10m
Durational – lasts until activated (see below)

A glowing sword of unearthly nature appears above the head of the target. This sword is ethereal and cannot be damaged or removed by physical means. It will continue to hang in the air above the target, moving as he moves, until activated by a command from the caster. It will then become solid and descend to strike the victim, emitting a metallic screech as it does so. Unless the sword is dodged (match its SPEED of 17 vs the target's EVASION), it will deal the hapless target a mighty blow. Use d10 + 2 for its Armour Bypass Roll; a successful hit inflicts 4d6 *HP* damage. After its single strike, successful or not, the sword vanishes.

If he chooses, the caster can make the sword's descent dependent on some condition. (Eg, 'Strike if I am slain.') It is thus an excellent spell for coercing an enemy. ('Kill me, and my *Sword of Damocles*'ll turn you into a kebab'!)

Sorcerer Spells of Level Seven (7 Magic Points to cast)

DEATHLIGHT

Match spell's SPEED of 16 vs targets' EVASION
Range: 40m

A very powerful bolt of energy leaps from the caster's hands, forking to strike 1 – 4 beings. A being failing to evade will take 3d6 + 10 *HP* damage (reduced by his/its Armour Factor, if any).

ENSLAVE

Match caster's MAGICAL ATTACK vs target's
MAGICAL DEFENCE
Range: 30m
Durational – Spell Expiry Roll applies

This more powerful variant on the *Command* spell will
affect a single being of any rank. A successful casting
renders the victim completely subservient to the
Sorcerer's will. Unlike *Command*, this spell turns its
victim into an unreasoning slave who will do only what
he is told. Language barriers are not a problem; the
victim will always understand what his master is
telling him to do, though with a tendency to follow
instructions literally – occasionally with unlooked-for
results. It takes one Combat Round to issue an *Enslaved*
character with orders, or to change existing orders.

NOVA

Match spell's SPEED of 18 vs targets' EVASION
Range: 5m

Myriad beams of searing light shoot from the caster's
body in all directions. Any being within 5m who fails to
jump clear is struck by 1 – 3 of the beams (roll d6: 1 – 2
= 1 beam, 3 – 4 = 2 beams, 5 – 6 = 3 beams). Each
beam inflicts 3d8 *HP* damage, less the target's Armour
Factor.

SPELL SCREEN

Durational – Spell Expiry Roll applies

This establishes a defensive enchantment around the
Sorcerer which will protect him from direct-attack
spells (ie those which involve a MAGICAL ATTACK vs
MAGICAL DEFENCE roll). The effect of the *Spell
Screen* is to reduce any spell passing into it by 5 *Magic*

Points. Unlike a *Wall of Magic*, the *Spell Screen* itself is not reduced in strength by this. (It is *not* possible to get a *Spell Screen* that filters out more than 5 MPs by expending more *Magic Points* in casting it. Also, the effects are not cumulative, so two *Spell Screens* are no better than one.)

Two special cases are worth considering. If a *Spell Screen* is overlapped with a *Wall of Magic*, attacking spells knock *Magic Points* off the *Wall* first, before being attenuated by the *Screen*. Secondly, the *Spell Screen* affects only spells cast at the Sorcerer himself, not spells cast at the *Screen*. Take the case of a Sorcerer who is wielding a *Vorpal Blade* and is protected by *Spell Screen*. A 12 MP *Dispel Magic* would be required to dispel the *Vorpal Blade*; but to deal with the *Screen*, only a 7 MP *Dispel Magic* would be needed.

STASIS

> Match caster's MAGICAL ATTACK vs target's MAGICAL DEFENCE
> Range: 20m
> Durational – lasts until Dispelled

The caster is able to 'freeze' 1 – 3 victims at an instant in Time. A character thus frozen will remain exactly where he was when he succumbed to the spell. He cannot think or act in any way (he is caught 'between ticks of the clock', as it were), nor can he be moved or harmed by any means while the *Stasis* is in effect.

VORPAL BLADE

> Durational – Spell Expiry Roll applies

In the caster's hand there appears a magic sword – as black as midnight, with a coruscating nimbus of green fire. This weapon is a + 3 sword. That is, it increases the Sorcerer's ATTACK and DEFENCE by 3 while he is fighting with it, uses 1d8 + 3 for Armour Bypass Rolls and does 7 *HP* damage on a successful strike. Putting this eldritch weapon down will cause it to vanish immediately. If the Sorcerer should be so foolish as to offer it to another, the sword will turn in his hand, strike him once, and then disappear forever!

Sorcerer Spells of Level Eight (8 Magic Points to cast)

ASTRAL GATE

Durational – (see below)

A shimmering portal, a rent in the very fabric of space itself, is created in front of the caster. This portal leads to any place the caster wishes to reach (not more than 150km away), allowing characters to cross this distance in the blink of an eye. The intended destination should be a spot which the caster knows reasonably well. If he is trying to reach a place he has only seen once, the caster has a 40% chance of 'missing' by up to a hundred metres (roll d100 for the distance out and d8 for direction – 1 = north, 2 = northeast, 3 = east, etc). If aiming for a destination he has never seen, and is guided only by another's account, the caster has a 50% chance of missing by up to a kilometre.

The *Astral Gate* will teleport only living beings and whatever they are wearing or carrying. It is not possible to lob a *Shadowbolt* through first, to take care of anyone at the far end! As each character passes through the *Gate*, a d6 is rolled. On a roll of 6, the spell expires. A Sorcerer must take three Combat Rounds to visualize his intended destination before casting *Astral Gate*. Unless he takes this precaution, there is a 60% chance that the far end of the Gate will emerge onto another plane of reality, and any character passing through will then be lost forever.

BASTION

Durational – Spell Expiry Roll applies

Motes of glittering light spread from the caster's hands and rapidly spread, 'painting' a surface in the air as they do. Within a second, an impenetrable steel-grey barrier has been created. This barrier has a maximum surface area of some 25 square metres, and may be made to form a hemisphere roughly 4m across (within which the Sorcerer may shelter while healing himself or casting more defensive spells) or a wall (blocking a dungeon corridor, perhaps, while the caster and his companions speed away from their foes).

BURDEN

Match spell's SPEED of 16 vs targets' EVASION
Range: 15m
Durational – Spell Expiry Roll applies

Cast at an area of ground, the Burden spell causes the pull of gravity to become so overwhelmingly strong that any being standing there will fall down and be unable to move until the spell expires. Very large creatures fare no better than smaller and weaker ones: 'the bigger they are. . .' The spell affects a circular area up to 5m across, extending upwards into the air no more than 3m. (It is not much use, therefore, against a flying creature.) The caster's enemies have a chance to jump clear when he casts the spell, and this is represented by matching the spell's SPEED against their EVASION scores. No such opportunity is available to those who blunder into the zone once the spell has taken effect, however; they are remorselessly pulled to the ground.

DESTRIER

Durational − (see below)

This conjuration is usable only at night, or in the light-less depths of an underworld, as it summons a demonic Warhorse which is driven back to its own fey world by the rays of the dawn. It will also vanish at once if the Sorcerer dismounts. The Destrier is a sere black steed clad in tarnished silver armour; its eyes burn with an emerald light. Any seeing it will know it to be a faerie beast, and characters of 1st − 3rd rank subtract 1 from ATTACK when fighting it. The *Destrier* can carry its master across a hundred kilometres of open country or woodland in a single night. It is fierce and terrible in battle, having an ATTACK of 17, DEFENCE of 4, EVASION of 4 and MAGICAL DEFENCE of 13. Its silver-shod hoofs and sharp teeth deal damage as a normal Warhorse but with + 1 on Armour Bypass Rolls. It has 2d6 + 12 *Health Points* and its silver barding gives it an Armour Factor of 3.

Note that it is only by this spell that a Sorcerer can ride a Warhorse. Normal Warhorses are available only to Knights and Barbarians.

EVIL EYE

Durational − Spell Expiry Roll applies

The caster of the spell becomes touched by the spirit of the Fomori demi-god, Balor, whose gaze is Death. The caster's left eye is filled with a fathomless dark. Any character meleeing him has a 40% chance of meeting the hideous stare of this eye. This check is made at the end of each Combat Round. (The chance may be less than 40% if the caster's opponent looks away or shuts his eyes − cf Basilisks). A character who looks into the eye's gaze is subject to a 1d12 fright attack: a twelve-sided die is rolled and the victim's rank is subtracted from the score. If the caster can roll less than or equal

40

to the result on 2d10, the victim dies.

The user of this spell temporarily loses sight in the affected eye. Thus deprived of binocular vision, he subtracts 1 point from ATTACK and 2 points from both DEFENCE and EVASION while the spell lasts.

RUNE

Durational – lasts until activated

This is a notorious spell used as a magical trap by high-ranking Sorcerers; experienced adventurers are always wary of stumbling across a Sorcerer's *Rune*. The *Rune* is cast by inscribing an occult symbol on a wall, flagstone, tapestry or other suitable object. The Sorcerer can then cast into it any other spell that he is able to use. This spell will be held by the *Rune* and released if anyone except the caster comes within 3m line of sight. The *Rune* must be exposed if it is to work, but Sorcerers can be quite artful in contriving abstract murals or odd locations (the ceiling? behind a door?) to keep others from noticing a *Rune* before it goes off. A Sorcerer may have only one *Rune* at any given time.

Sorcerer Spells of Level Nine (9 Magic Points to cast)

ANIMATE BONES

Range: touch

By casting this over the skeletal remains of some unfortunate whom he himself slew, the Sorcerer can cause them to rise up as a Skeleton. It makes no difference what skills the being possessed in life, for this spell does not restore the original soul or intellect. The Skeleton is merely a simple-minded creature whose main virtue lies in total obedience to its animator. All Skeletons thus have the same abilities: ATTACK 10, DEFENCE 5, EVASION 3, MAGICAL DEFENCE 3 and 2 – 7 Health Points (roll 1d6 + 1).

41

BATTLEMASTER

Durational – Spell Expiry Roll applies

A supernatural, obsidian-armoured warrior is summoned from another Plane and bound in the caster's service for the period of the spell. The *Battlemaster* is clad in magical chainmail and wields a magic axe. His characteristics and scores are:

Strength 18	ATTACK 30	Axe (d8 + 2, 8 points)
Reflexes 13	DEFENCE 24	Armour Factor 6
24 Health Points	MAGICAL DEFENCE 17 EVASION 8	

When the spell runs out, the *Battlemaster* returns to his own dimensional Plane, where any wounds he has received are supernaturally healed before the next time he is summoned. Although any given Sorcerer can materialize the *Battlemaster* only once per day, he exists on many planes simultaneously and it is thus possible for two Sorcerers actually to summon him at the same time. If the *Battlemaster* should be ordered to attack himself (ie, 'another' *Battlemaster* summoned by a different Sorcerer), his two selves will merge into one and he will be freed from the control of either summoner. He will then proceed to wreak havoc before returning to his own world.

FIRESTORM

Match spell's SPEED of 18 vs targets' EVASION
Range: 30m

The caster flings a ball of snarling flames which explodes into an inferno of 6m diameter. Characters will take 4d10 + 4 *HP* damage if they fail to jump clear – and 4 *HP* damage even if they do, simply from the peripheral heat of this terrible blast! A target wearing magic armour (of any sort) may reduce the damage he takes by 3 points; unenchanted armour provides no defence.

INVISIBILITY

Durational – Spell Expiry Roll applies

The caster is rendered invisible. If his opponents are aware of his general location (perhaps he sneezed or knocked over a vase), he may be attacked with spells. Direct-attack spells affect an invisible target normally, but indirect-attack spells are subject to a penalty of 1d8 SPEED points to represent their likelihood of being slightly off-target. A character attempting to melee the invisible Sorcerer incurs a penalty of – 4 from ATTACK and – 8 from DEFENCE (just like fighting blind, of course – see Book One). Missile weapons are almost useless against one who is invisible: the bowman halves his normal ATTACK and subtracts 3. Sir Balin, who has an ATTACK of 13, therefore shoots at an invisible enemy as though with an ATTACK of only 4.

MIRACLE CURE

Range: 5m

This spell restores the recipient to his normal *Health Point* score, cures any diseases and eradicates any toxins he is suffering from, and regenerates any missing limbs or organs. As with the *Lesser Healing* and *Greater Healing* spells, it has no effect on a dead character.

RAISE FOG

Durational – Spell Expiry Roll applies

With the casting of this spell (which must be used out-of-doors), a dense mist quickly rises to cover an area

60m across by 5m high. This area is centred on the Sorcerer's position when he cast the spell. The Sorcerer himself can see quite normally within the *Fog*, but for others the visibility is barely 3m.

Sorcerer Spells of Level Ten (10 Magic Points to cast)

DOPPELGANGER

A soulless duplicate of a person known to the caster can be created. The caster must first fashion a simulacrum of clay mixed with his own blood. This blood can never be replenished, and the caster's normal *Health Points* score is permanently reduced by 1d4 points as a consequence. After making the simulacrum, the caster must acquire some item often used or worn by the person he is trying to duplicate. A favourite cloak would do, or a sword. With such an item in his possession, the Sorcerer casts the spell and his simulacrum arises in the likeness of the original. The *Doppelganger* has the physical characteristics and skills (including fighting ability) of the character it resembles, but not his knowledge skills. It is a being without reason or volition, and will simply obey its creator's commands without question. Having no soul, it cannot walk on consecrated ground and will not cast a reflection.

HECATOMB

Match caster's MAGICAL ATTACK vs victims' MAGICAL DEFENCE

This spell is applied to all beings, whether friend or foe, within 10m of the caster. It is instant death for any on whom it takes effect. So potent an attack is not without its cost. The spell causes a severe magical backlash to its caster, represented by the loss of 1 – 100 *experi-*

ence points. It is a price few Sorcerers would be prepared to pay, except in the most extreme circumstances.

PENTACLE OF ENTRAPMENT

> Match caster's MAGICAL ATTACK vs victims' MAGICAL DEFENCE
> Durational – lasts three days (and see below)

This spell requires a large pentacle about 5m across to be drawn or engraved. When the spell is cast, the pentacle becomes a trap for the caster's enemies. The first 2 – 12 beings of up to 5th rank to come within 20m (they must be able to see the pentacle) are subject to the spell. Those on whom it takes effect will be instantaneously transported within the pentacle's boundary. Though unharmed, they will be powerless to escape unless they know the 'key' word (arbitrarily chosen by the Sorcerer when he cast the spell) which unlocks the *Pentacle of Entrapment*. The spell is also negated if any part of the pentacle design is erased, but this cannot be accomplished by one trapped within it.

RESURRECT

> Range: touch

This spell will restore life to a character who has been dead for no more than one lunar month (twenty-eight days). The revitalized character permanently loses 1d3 *Health Points*, and for a week after rising from the dead his *Strength* and *Reflexes* are half normal.

Resurrect must be cast at sunrise, and the effort of employing it renders the caster unable to use any spells above the fifth level for the rest of the day. This means that Sorcerers are usually very reluctant to cast *Resurrect*, whatever their rank. Even if persuaded to do so, the Sorcerer is likely to charge at least two hundred Gold Pieces for his service.

SCRY

Durational – lasts three minutes

This enables the Sorcerer to look into a specially-prepared obsidian mirror (his 'Speculum') and call up images of people, far off places and past events. If asked to show a place, the mirror will show only a general view, not a specific location. 'Show me the tower of Mizar the magician' would bring a view of the building's exterior. The Sorcerer can then move his scrying viewpoint around, but not through physical barriers such as walls and closed doors, nor onto consecrated ground. The mirror transmits images only; the Sorcerer can hear nothing of what is said by those he spies upon. An observed Sorcerer or Mystic of equal or greater rank will know when another descries him, and may use *Dispel Magic* to cancel the spell (this also causes the Speculum to shatter).

When the Sorcerer desires to look on past events, he must know the time when the event in question took place to within twelve hours. If he has some object which was on the scene at the time he wishes to view, such knowledge is unnecessary.

(Constructing the mirror needed for this spell will cost the Sorcerer 30 – 180 (3d6 × 10) Gold Pieces. He may not then construct a second Speculum unless and until the first shatters.)

TRANSFORMATION

Durational – lasts three minutes

The caster may alter his form to become any creature whose rank-equivalent does not exceed his rank. His *Health Points* and MAGICAL ATTACK and MAGICAL DEFENCE scores are unaffected by the change, but his fighting skills become those of the new form. Note that the Sorcerer acquires only the physical abilities of his new form, not the magical ones. If Limorien *Trans-*

forms himself into a Gorgon, his hair will turn to deadly snakes but he will not get the monster's petrifying stare.

A Sorcerer cannot use magic while in altered form, unless the form is of a creature which is basically humanoid so that he can make the necessary hand-gestures.

Transformation lasts three minutes (= 30 Combat Rounds), though the caster may of course terminate it before then if need be.

Other Skills of a Sorcerer

Sorcerers do not rely only on their innate ability to cast spells. A study of sorcery imparts the techniques needed to prepare scrolls, potions and minor magical items. A high-ranking Sorcerer will go adventuring with a small arsenal of such magical adjuncts.

CALLIGRAPHY

This is the ability to prepare magical scrolls, a skill known to any Sorcerer of 4th rank or higher. The total cost of the basic materials for a scroll will be 3 – 18 Crowns: parchment of high quality is called for, along with gold leaf and some rare and expensive pigments. The scroll may be for any spell that the Sorcerer is able to cast (that is, whose level does not exceed his rank), and the maximum number of *Magic Points* placed in the spell is limited by the Sorcerer's rank. An 8th rank character could not write out a scroll for a 9 *MP* Wall of Magic, even though he could personally cast the spell at three times that strength. The process of inscribing and illuminating a scroll takes a full lunar month (twenty-eight days).

Each scroll that a Sorcerer prepares temporarily suppresses 2 points of his normal *Magic Points* score until it is used. A 10th rank Sorcerer with five scrolls at his belt would thus have 25 *MPs* instead of his usual 35.

ALCHEMY

Alchemy is the science which governs the preparation of potions and thaumaturgic compounds. A Sorcerer first begins to master this skill when he reaches 6th rank.

A fully equipped laboratory, which can be established at a cost of some two hundred Crowns, is the first prerequisite. This comprises a lot of equipment, so the Sorcerer must have somewhere to set it all up. If he later needs to relocate his laboratory (maybe the locals think he's doing something unholy), 2 – 20 Crowns of the set-up cost can be salvaged in the form of small portable items and ingredients.

The Sorcerer does not become a Master Alchemist overnight. At 6th rank he knows how to distil only the less complex potions. Others must wait until he gains more experience:

Sorcerer's rank	Potions which can be prepared (with ingredients cost)
6th	Dexterity (35C), Occult Acuity (40C), Strength (35C)
7th	above plus: Healing (40C), Replenishment (100C), Poison (120C), Theriac (100C)
8th	above plus: Night Vision (35C), Smoke (50C), Amianthus Dust (150C)
9th	above plus: Control (120C), Truth (100C), Love (100C), Sleep (200C)
10th	above plus: Transformation (200C), Dreams (200C), the Elemental Essences (200C), Evaporating Potion (200C), Elixir Vitae (250C), Virus Lunare (180C)

It takes twenty-eight days to distil a potion. In a normal sized laboratory there could be up to ten potions 'on the boil' at one time. The Sorcerer cannot leave these bubbling away while he goes off on an adventure; the alchemical process calls for continual supervision as various ingredients are mixed and added, vaporized, condensed and filtered.

There is always a chance that the Sorcerer will do something wrong or miss out some vital ingredient. This gets less likely as his experience grows. The chance that a potion will turn out misbrewed and useless is 40% when the Sorcerer is 6th rank, decreasing by 10% per rank above the 6th. This roll is made by the GamesMaster; the Sorcerer only finds out whether he got the formula right when he (or someone else) drinks it.

Full details of the various potions are given in Chapter Five.

ARTIFICE

This is the skill involved in constructing magic amulets, talismans and rings. It is a very precise science, and there is only a very slight chance (5%) that the item will turn out flawed or useless. The work of constructing magic items is intensely demanding and ties up most of the Sorcerer's occult energy over a long period. No adventuring is possible while making one of these items. If the Sorcerer has to cast any spells, he must make sure he keeps back at least 20 *Magic Points* each day to fuel his laboratory enchantments. Even breaking off the work for one day is enough to undo these vital enchantments, and the entire procedure must then start again from scratch. A Sorcerer who is engaged in making a magic item will not appreciate any interruptions.

Talismans may be constructed when the Sorcerer reaches 8th rank. The work will take seven months and cost the Sorcerer in the region of 300 Crowns.

Amulets must wait until the Sorcerer reaches 10th rnak. Manufacture of one of these items will take a year and a day, at a basic materials cost of 400 to 500 Crowns.

Only a Master Sorcerer of 12th rank or above is able to construct a magic *ring*. Apparatus and miscellaneous costs are likely to be in the region of 600 Crowns. The work will take three years; those rings which have charges will also require one month per charge.

It is said that at 15th rank a Sorcerer has such consummate understanding of Artifice that he is able to build magic items of his own devising, rather than copying the powers and procedures handed down in the ancient lore. If any player-character should ever attain this lofty pinnacle, it it up to you as Games-Master to set the final ruling on this. As a general rule, Artifice (and all other Sorcerous skills) is in a very muddy state compared to the organized bodies of knowledge that began to develop by the 16th century. Dozens of arbitrary and half-true theories circulate. The medieval culture of our DRAGON WARRIORS world has not evolved the modern 'scientific method', so Sorcerers tend to make new discoveries in an entirely haphazard fashion. Developing an innovation in the field is quite extraordinary, as it would never occur to most medieval Sorcerers to go beyond the tested arcana of centuries past. A Sorcerer who undertakes something new may be starting on a lifetime's work. Players should understand this.

3 Mystics

Minimum Requirements

To be a Mystic, a character must have a Psychic Talent score of at least 9. There is no minimum Intelligence requirement — Mysticism, unlike Sorcery, is not academically demanding.

Casting Spells

The spells are categorized into levels of increasing power and complexity, and a Mystic cannot use spells of a higher level than his rank. Whenever a Mystic casts a spell, he must make a check to see whether the effort 'psychically fatigues' him. To avoid psychic fatigue, the Mystic must roll equal to or less than

$$13 + \text{his rank} - \text{spell's level}$$

on 1d20. This is called the *Psychic Fatigue Check*. If it fails, the Mystic cannot cast any more spells that day. Mystics automatically recover from psychic fatigue at dawn.

Note that when making the Psychic Fatigue Check, a roll of 20 always results in fatigue, whatever the Mystic's rank or the level of the spell he's casting.

EXAMPLE

Caedmon Skysoul, a 2nd rank Mystic, casts *Invigorate*, which is a level one spell. He therefore needs to roll 14 or less on d20 to avoid psychic fatigue. In fact he rolls an 18. Caedmon now cannot cast spells until the following dawn (although this does not prevent the *Invigorate* he just cast from taking effect).

Casting Spells Above Their Level

For the purpose of penetrating the sorcerous defences *Wall of Magic* and *Spell Screen*, Mystic spells are considered to have a 'Magic Point strength' equal to their level. Thus (even though Mystics do not use *Magic Points*), an *Enthrall* spell, being of level four, is equivalent in strength to a 4 *MP* Sorcerer spell such as *Curse*.

Sorcerers may put extra *Magic Points* into a spell to help it 'punch through' magical defences. Mystics cannot do that, but they *can* choose to cast a spell above its normal level. This increases the chance of psychic fatigue but gives a more powerful spell. As an example, consider Shugendo Sai, a Mystic who is about to attack an enemy Sorcerer. Suspecting that his foe has put up a 4 *MP Wall of Magic*, Shugendo Sai casts his *Enthrall* as an eighth level spell. He makes his Psychic Fatigue Check just as though he had cast a level eight spell. His *Enthrall* – after losing the equivalent of 4 *Magic Points* to the *Wall* – is reduced to fourth level and attacks the Sorcerer normally.

Mystics and Armour

Like Sorcerers, Mystics are not really at home in a heavy suit of armour. Their style of combat is unsuited to such encumbrance, resulting in combat penalties (see DRAGON WARRIORS 1, Chapter Three).

Moreover, enchanted armour of any sort serves to impede the Mystic's link with the universal psychic flow (the 'Force').

Magical armour bonus	Chance of bungled spell
+ 1	10%
+ 2	20%
+ 3	30%

A Mystic who bungles a spell must make his Psychic Fatigue Check as though he had managed to cast it, though in fact the spell simply fails to operate.

Terminating a Spell

A Mystic can cancel out his own durational spells at any time. Unlike a Sorcerer, the Mystic does not need to take a Combat Round to do this. He can cause any or all of his durational spells to lapse just by not bothering to sustain them.

If a Mystic is killed or knocked unconscious, any durational spells he has going at the time will expire immediately.

Sorcerers rarely leave Spell Expiry durational spells going after a combat, as they prefer to recoup some of their expended *Magic Points* (see Chapter Two). A Mystic gains nothing by prematurely terminating a spell, and will usually choose to leave it going until it expires naturally. It is, however, not convenient for players or the GM to have to make a Spell Expiry Roll for every six seconds of game-time when there is no longer a combat in progress. You may prefer to make a minute-by-minute roll to see when the spell wears off. The chance that the spell will still be operating after one minute is 75% (which is statistically equivalent to ten successive Spell Expiry Rolls). Thus, the spellcaster rolls d100 for every minute that elapses after combat is over; on a roll of 01 – 75, his spell remains on for another minute before he need roll again.

EXAMPLE

Caedmon increases his strength with a *Might* spell while battling a Mummy. The spell has not worn off several Rounds later when, with the combat over and the Mummy defeated, Caedmon's fellows begin to discuss which area of the underworld to explore next.

Caedmon does not wish to cancel his *Might* spell, but the GM does not want to disrupt the flow of the game by having him make a Spell Expiry Roll for every six seconds the characters stand around talking. Instead, he has Caedmon's player roll on d100 every minute. He manages to roll under 76 three times in a row, so Caedmon's strength is still magically enhanced three minutes later when another Mummy chances upon the still-arguing characters. A battle ensues, and Caedmon resumes making his Spell Expiry Roll on a Round-by-Round basis. . .

CHARACTER CREATION SUMMARY – Mystics

A. *Strength, Reflexes, Intelligence, Psychic Talent* and *Looks*: roll 3d6 for each
(*Psychic Talent* must be at least 9 if character is to qualify as a Mystic)

B. *Health Points*: roll 1d6 + 5

C. Basic ATTACK 12, DEFENCE 6

D. Basic MAGICAL ATTACK 14, MAGICAL DEFENCE 4

E. Basic EVASION 3

F. Initially equipped with lantern, flint-&-tinder, backpack, bow, quiver containing six arrows, dagger, ring mail armour, 2 – 20 Florins, sword or staff.

(See also DRAGON WARRIORS 1, Chapter Two: Creating a Character. This will explain how to modify the basic scores given above if the Mystic has non-average characteristics.)

CHARACTER SHEET

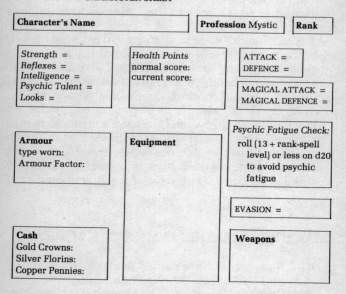

| Character's Name | Profession Mystic | Rank |

Strength =
Reflexes =
Intelligence =
Psychic Talent =
Looks =

Health Points
normal score:
current score:

ATTACK =
DEFENCE =

MAGICAL ATTACK =
MAGICAL DEFENCE =

Armour
type worn:
Armour Factor:

Equipment

Psychic Fatigue Check:
roll (13 + rank–spell
    level) or less on d20
    to avoid psychic
    fatigue

EVASION =

Cash
Gold Crowns:
Silver Florins:
Copper Pennies:

Weapons

Each player will require a blank Character Sheet. Permission is granted to make photocopies.

The Spells

These are the spells usable by Mystics. Remember that the Mystic's rank sets the upper limit on the level of spells he can cast.

Spells of Level One

INVIGORATE
MIRAGE
SEE ENCHANTMENT
SUSPENDED
   ANIMATION

Spells of Level Two

DARKSIGHT
DAZZLE
MIGHT
PURSUIT

Spells of Level Three

ALLSEEING EYE
MIND CLOAK
NOURISH
TELEKINESIS

Spells of Level Four

CLAIRVOYANCE
ENTHRALL
HIDDEN TARGET
TELEPATHY

Spells of Level Five

FORCE FIELD
MYSTIC BLAST
PASS UNSEEN
TRUTHSENSE

Spells of Level Six

ASSESSMENT
PURIFICATION
STEEL CLAW
SURVIVAL

Spells of Level Seven

DUEL
LEVITATION
PARALYSIS
PROTECTION

Spells of Level Eight

INTANGIBILITY
MINDPOOL
SWIFTNESS
TRANCE

Spells of Level Nine

IMPREGNABLE
   SPHERE
PHOENIX
TELEPORT
THUNDERCLAP

Mystic Spells of Level One

INVIGORATE

The Mystic converts psychic energy into physical energy, releasing a powerful restorative force into his body. He regains two *Health Points*. The spell will not increase his *Health Point* score above its normal level, of course.

MIRAGE

Range: 10m
Durational – Spell Expiry Roll applies

A visual illusion is created, of anything the caster wishes so long as it is no bigger than man-sized. The *Mirage* can be 'programmed' to perform a set of actions (eg, a guard marching up and down outside a door) or it can be controlled mentally, like a holographic puppet. There is a 10% chance that the *Mirage* will be recognized as such at first glance.

SEE ENCHANTMENT

Durational – Spell Expiry Roll applies

While this spell is in effect, the Mystic is able to see powerful concentrations of magic energy. He could tell whether a weapon or talisman were magical, but would not be able to sense impermanent enchantments (such as the presence of a *Command* spell).

SUSPENDED ANIMATION

The Mystic is able to sink into a deep coma, outwardly resembling death. This coma lasts for any preset duration up to a year and a day. Even ESP will detect no thoughts, but in fact the Mystic does remain aware of his surroundings – except that his mental processes are slowed by a factor of sixty.

Mystic Spells of Level Two

DARKSIGHT

Durational – Spell Expiry Roll applies

The Mystic acquires the ability to see in darkness like an Elf. That is, he can see with perfect clarity by moonlight or under a star-filled night sky, and in the pitch dark of an underworld as though it were deep twilight.

DAZZLE

This spell produces a flash of brilliant light that will all but blind any sighted creature within 5m for one full Combat Round. This gives the Mystic the chance to escape from his foes or make one free strike while they are dazzled (and hence – 8 from DEFENCE).

MIGHT

Durational – Spell Expiry Roll applies

A powerful spell for use in combat, this has the effect of increasing the Mystic's *Strength*. If his normal *Strength* score is 15 or less, it temporarily increases to 16; if normally 16 or more, it increases to 19.

PURSUIT

Durational – lasts one day

This enables the Mystic to follow the psychic spoor of a person or creature whom he knows or has had described to him. He may thus track his quarry over terrain of any sort, and in all weathers.

Mystic Spells of Level Three

ALLSEEING EYE

Durational – Spell Expiry Roll applies

This extends the Mystic's power of vision beyond the visible spectrum, enabling him to perceive any invisible object or being within 10m. The Mystic sees the invisible shapes as featureless silhouettes.

MIND CLOAK

Durational – lasts ten minutes

This spell puts up a psionic shield around the Mystic, preventing detection by ESP, *Scry* or similar magical means. If the caster is being tracked by another Mystic using the *Pursuit* spell, this spell will cause the latter to lose his 'scent'.

NOURISH

This spell ensures the Mystic need never starve when he has no food or water. A single casting provides him with refreshment and nourishment for a full day.

TELEKINESIS

Range: 25m
Durational – Spell Expiry Roll applies

This is the classic parapsychic ability to move and manipulate objects at a distance by the power of the mind. The spell affects a single object of up to 0.5kg weight. The maximum velocity at which an object can be moved by *Telekinesis* is about 15m per Combat Round, making for a rather ineffective missile (SPEED

8 to dodge, and doing no appreciable damage on impact anyway). The Mystic may wield a dagger by *Telekinesis*, in order to melee an opponent at a distance; he would do so with half his normal ATTACK (*Telekinetic* control is quite clumsy) and doing 1 *HP* less damage for a successful blow (because there is little strength in the spell).

Mystic Spells of Level Four

CLAIRVOYANCE

Durational – Spell Expiry Roll applies

This spell intensifies the Mystic's inherent paranormal senses, and so confers the ability to see anything within 5m even through solid objects. A full 360° arc of 'vision' is obtained, making it very difficult to take the Mystic unawares.

ENTHRALL

Match caster's MAGICAL ATTACK vs target's MAGICAL DEFENCE
Range: 5m
Durational – Spell Expiry Roll applies

If successful, this spell warps its victim's judgement so that he believes the Mystic to be his friend. This delusion does not destroy the victim's loyalty to his real friends, however, and neither does it make him well-disposed towards the Mystic's companions. He will believe anything the Mystic tells him and, unless the Mystic openly attacks him, will trust him completely until the spell wears off.

HIDDEN TARGET

Durational – Spell Expiry Roll applies

This spell enables the Mystic to pick off targets with arrow, sling or thrown dagger even if blindfolded. He ignores the usual penalties for poor visibility. Even in thick fog, or if the target is invisible, the Mystic shoots as if he could see him perfectly. He must know there is someone to shoot at, though – he cannot just walk into a room and lob off a few arrows 'on spec' in case there should happen to be an invisible Sorcerer about.

TELEPATHY

Range: 10km
Durational – lasts ten minutes

The Mystic is able to communicate telepathically with another (who must be known to him) over considerable distances. Communication is in the form of images as well as words, so different languages need not prove an insurmountable obstacle. Note, however, that two characters from totally different cultures (a medieval wizard and an Inca priest, for instance) may be simply unable to think in the same terms.

Mystic Spells of Level Five

FORCE FIELD

Durational – Spell Expiry Roll applies (and see below)

This spell protects the Mystic with a thin, invisible force barrier. When a blow is struck against him, the Force Field absorbs the damage and prevents it from harming him. Once it has absorbed a total of 15 *HP* damage, the *Force Field* collapses. It gives no protection from magical weapons, spells or other forms of attack (such as flames or poisonous fumes).

MYSTIC BLAST

Match spell's SPEED of 16 vs target's EVASION
Range: 30m

This takes the form of a psychic force bolt. If it strikes its target, the bolt inflicts 3d6 + 1 *HP* damage. The target may reduce this damage by his Armour Factor, if any. (A character in chainmail would take only 3d6 − 3 *HP*, for example.)

PASS UNSEEN

Durational − Spell Expiry Roll applies

The Mystic becomes invisible. . . up to a point. He can walk right past his enemies and they will not notice him. This is not as good as true *Invisibility* (the high-level Sorcerer variety) because he will still reflect in a mirror, and turns visible at once if he tries to attack anybody or casts another spell. Also, the spell will only fool beings of 1st to 4th rank/rank-equivalent.

TRUTHSENSE

Durational − Spell Expiry Roll applies

While the spell lasts, the Mystic is able to tell with 85% accuracy when someone is lying to him. That is, if a character tells him a lie, 1d100 is rolled. On a roll of 01 − 85, he knows it to be a lie. On a roll of 86 − 00, he is not sure one way or the other. The d100 roll is made secretly by the GamesMaster, for obvious reasons.

Mystic Spells of Level Six

ASSESSMENT

Range: 10m

By means of this spell, the Mystic can instantaneously assess all characters within range and determine the following: their Profession, rank (or rank-equivalent) and current *Health Points*. *Assessment* is blocked by *Mind Cloak*, and will not give any information about characters above 10th rank.

PURIFICATION

This spell cleanses the Mystic's body of all ailments and poisons, and heals up to 8 *Health Points* if he is wounded.

STEEL CLAW

Durational – Spell Expiry Roll applies

The caster's hand is transformed into a rigid talon of gleaming metal. When he strikes with this in combat, he uses a d12 for Armour Bypass Rolls and inflicts 8 *HP* damage with each successful blow.

SURVIVAL

Durational – lasts one day

The Mystic is able to endure extremes of heat and cold such as might be experienced under a blazing desert sky or in an arctic waste. He is *not* protected from direct exposure to fire. *Survival* also enables the Mystic to go without air for up to an hour after drawing a single breath.

Mystic Spells of Level Seven

DUEL

Durational – (see below)

To use this spell, the Mystic must close in melee with an opponent. The spell shifts both the Mystic and his opponent out of phase with the rest of the universe; they remain visible only as a flickering, indistinct blur. Out-of-phase characters are on another plane, and cannot affect (or be affected by) their surroundings. Unable to move from the spot where they 'phased out', the two combatants must continue their battle until one is slain. Only then does the spell terminate, returning them – alive or dead – to the normal world.

LEVITATION

Durational – Spell Expiry Roll applies (and see below)

This spell allows the caster to rise up into the air and float around. *Levitational* movement is quite slow – only 10m per Combat Round (normal walking speed, in other words). This spell requires concentration to sustain. If the Mystic wants to enter melee or cast another spell, he must first cancel the *Levitation*.

PARALYSIS

Match caster's MAGICAL ATTACK vs target's MAGICAL DEFENCE
Range: 15m
Durational – Spell Expiry Roll applies

This spell, if it takes effect, results in paralysis of all the voluntary muscles. It will work only on a living being. The victim collapses at once, but remains conscious. Another Mystic affected by this spell could still cast spells of his own, since Mystics need only the power of their psyche to work magic and do not rely on the chants and arcane gestures of the Sorcerer.

PROTECTION

Durational – lasts until Dispelled (and see below)

A potent spell which adds 2 points to the caster's MAGICAL DEFENCE and increases his Armour Factor by 2. The caster can sustain this indefinitely if he chooses to, but he must add + 1 to the die roll whenever he makes a Psychic Fatigue Check while the *Protection* spell is in effect.

Mystic Spells of Level Eight

INTANGIBILITY

Durational – Spell Expiry Roll applies

The Mystic, and any items he is wearing or carrying, become intangible. He can pass through solid objects as though they were not there. While *Intangible*, a magical weapon is required to hit him in combat. Indirect-attack spells like *Firestorm* pass harmlessly through his insubstantial form, though direct-attack spells are still fully effective. The Mystic must take great care when using this spell – if it expires while he is inside a solid object, he will die.

MINDPOOL

Range: 3m
Durational – lasts thirty seconds (5 Combat Rounds)

This spell enables two Mystics to combine their power

for a brief time. With multiple castings of the spell, more Mystics can be included in the *Mindpool* – up to five individuals at one time. Mystics in a *Mindpool* each resist hostile direct-attack spells with the total MAGICAL DEFENCE of the whole group, and each casts his own spells with the highest MAGICAL ATTACK of the group.

Example: Two Mystics have reached the main burial chamber within an ancient barrow. Suddenly they are aware of thin cloaked shapes loping towards them from the darkness. Wights! The senior Mystic casts Mindpool, linking himself with his 4th rank companion. They now add their MAGICAL DEFENCE scores together: 7 + 12 in this case, so each now has an effective MAGICAL DEFENCE of 19. The 4th rank Mystic is still only able to cast spells up to level four – but that includes the direct-attack spell *Enthrall*, which he can now cast with his companion's MAGICAL ATTACK of 21.

SWIFTNESS

Durational – Spell Expiry Roll applies

This accelerates the caster's metabolism and speeds his physical movements. He gets two actions of his own to every one Combat Round experienced by those around him. The first of these actions must be taken at the very start of each CR, and the second at the point in the CR (determined by his *Reflexes* score) when he would normally get to act. The actions might be two 10m moves, or a move and an attack, or any other combination of actions. What the Mystic *cannot* do is cast two spells in one CR. This is because he continues to think at the normal rate.

TRANCE

Durational – lasts ten minutes

The Mystic enters a trance-like state while his psychic self, or *ka*, is freed from his body and is able to travel up to five kilometres away. The *ka* can see and hear, but is ethereal and cannot interact with or be seen by others. However, if it comes into the presence of a character of equal or higher rank then the latter will be able to sense it. Another Mystic could then use *Pursuit* to trace the *ka* back to its body.

Mystic Spells of Level Nine

IMPREGNABLE SPHERE

Durational – Spell Expiry Roll applies

The Mystic is surrounded by an invisible force bubble that blocks all physical attacks: missiles, creatures, indirect-attack spells, etc. Attacks of this type can pass neither into *nor out of* the *Impregnable Sphere*. Direct-attack spells (ie, those which entail a MAGICAL ATTACK vs MAGICAL DEFENCE roll) are not impeded. The *Sphere* will not move around, so the Mystic must remain in one spot while the spell lasts.

PHOENIX

This spell allows the Mystic to return from the dead. He (or, more accurately, his spirit-self) must cast it the Combat Round after he is slain. The body immediately begins to smoulder and then burn fiercely; no natural means can douse this blaze. After 5 Combat Rounds (thirty seconds), the Mystic arises from his own ashes like the majestic bird of legend. All his wounds are healed by the spell, but his *Health Point* score is per-

manently reduced by 1 point. The same fire that revivi-
fies him will also destroy any equipment that was on
his body – only certain exceptional magic items may
survive, and this is at the GamesMaster's discretion.
This spell cannot be cast more than once a week.

TELEPORT

By using this spell, the Mystic can vanish and reappear
at another point within 100m. He can only teleport to
somewhere he has been before, or which is in his line-
of-sight when he casts the spell.

THUNDERCLAP

Match spell's SPEED of 12 vs target's EVASION
Range: 1m

The Mystic can blow a wall down with one shout! In
fact, the shout is a focus for the immense destructive
energy of the psyche. If directed at an opponent who
fails to jump clear, the spell inflicts 6d6 + 6 *HP*
damage. Unenchanted armour gives no protection
from this, and even enchanted armour absorbs only 2
HP. The *Thunderclap* can be used to smash a 2m wide
hole in stone walls up to half a metre thick.

Other Abilities of a Mystic

Constant training in the use of the mind's power provides the Mystic with other abilities besides his spells.
The supernormal senses that are latent in all of us are
awakened in him. Although not fully reliable, they are
indispensible aids on any adventure for, in contrast to
his spells, the Mystic can use them over and over without suffering psychic fatigue.
At higher ranks, Mystics acquire the gift of manu-

facturing enchanted arms and armour. Any item reflects the man (or woman) who created it, and the spiritual perfection and enlightenment of the adept Mystic shows in the wondrous weaponry he makes. Mystics themselves are rarely known to use magic armour (we have already seen how it impedes their spellcasting), but they have no problem with magic weapons. As well as crafting items for his own use, the Mystic may choose to make them 'to order' for characters of other Professions. Strictly speaking, there is nothing to stop him from setting up shop as an artisan and churning out one magic weapon after another. He could obviously turn a tidy profit this way, but it would not really be in keeping with the true mystical Way. Each item that a Mystic makes should be unique, fashioned with a specific owner in mind (even if that person is not the one who eventually gets to use it). This restriction is not inherent in the DRAGON WARRIORS rules; it is left to the player to role-play his Mystic character accurately.

PREMONITION (or SIXTH SENSE)

This is the ability to sense danger. It must be applied to a specific object or location within 5m of the Mystic. It does not give any exact knowledge as to the form of the danger. (A door which registered as dangerous could be booby-trapped – or it might have a Vampire lurking on the other side of it!)

The chance of perceiving danger (if there is any danger to be perceived) is

$$35\% + 2\%/\text{rank}$$

So Caedmon Skysoul, who is 2nd rank, has a Premonition success rate of 39%.

To use Premonition, the Mystic must first concentrate on the place or thing under suspicion. This takes two full Combat Rounds while he clears his mind of all distractions. In the third CR, the GamesMaster rolls d100. If the roll comes up within the Mystic's success range, the GM informs him of any danger that is present. If the percentile roll is outside the required range, or if there is in fact no danger, the Mystic simply gets no impression. (Note that the Mystic will not be able to distinguish between sensing 'no danger' and not sensing 'danger'.)

Would it not be possible to double check a Premonition reading by waiting another two Combat Rounds and trying again? In fact, no. Having got a negative reading (for whatever reason) the Mystic will continue to get that same reading on every attempt until the circumstances actually change in some way (eg, the brook he's previously checked out as safe is suddenly poisoned by some Goblins upstream).

ESP (or SEVENTH SENSE)

This is the ability to detect thoughts within a range of 10m. No indication is given of direction, nor of the number of beings – although the Mystic is able to selectively 'tune out' the thoughts of his companions. He can tell the difference between intelligent thoughts and animal thoughts, but he cannot actually read minds.

The success chance of ESP is

$$05\% + 3\%/\text{rank}$$

Looking at Caedmon again, we see his ESP ability is at 11%.

The Mystic must prepare for three Combat Rounds before attempting to use ESP. Unlike Premonition, this does not take all his concentration. He could be in the middle of a fight and still use his ESP ability. The percentile roll is made, as before, by the GM.

A Mystic using *Mind Cloak* will not register on ESP. Nor will the following: Elves (except if detected by an Elven Mystic), Ghosts, Gnomes, Goblins, Hobgoblins and the Undead. Tenebrous and obscure, the thoughts of these magic folk slip through the Human Mystic's coarse ESP net.

A Mystic of 9th rank or higher will always be able to sense the proximity of another Mystic of 9th rank or higher (unless the latter has got a *Mind Cloak* spell up). The Mystic Force is so strong with such individuals that they activate one another's Seventh Sense automatically.

ENCHANTMENT OF ARMS & ARMOUR

A 4th rank Mystic is able to produce + 1 magic weapons. At 6th rank the ability extends to + 2 items, and at 9th rank to + 3 items. (See Chapter Five, ENCHANTED ARMOUR and ENCHANTED WEAPONS for explanation of these terms.)

Producing an enchanted weapon or suit of armour entails more than just stoking up a forge and hammering out the metal. A long period of solitude and fasting, of physical and mental preparation, must come first. The task may take months or years:

Item	Time taken to create
+ 1 arrow or quarrel	25 days
+ 2 arrow or quarrel	125 days
+ 3 arrow or quarrel	375 days
+ 1 weapon	100 days
+ 2 weapon	500 days
+ 3 weapon	1500 days
+ 1 armour (any sort)	100 days
+ 2 armour (any sort)	400 days
+ 3 armour (any sort)	900 days

If the Mystic fails to remain in the proper transcendent state throughout, he may produce a flawed item. Obviously, the chance of this diminishes as the Mystic becomes more dedicated and more accomplished – as he advances in rank, in other words. The chance of producing a flawed item is 40% at 4th rank, 30% at 5th, etc. In the case of a Mystic player-character, the player himself, not the GM, makes this roll. A Mystic always knows when he has made a flawed item. Flawed items will function normally if used, but there is a general aura of imperfection and possibly evil about them. This will detect as dangerous under Premonition. Eventually, the flawed item will bring ill-luck to its owner by embroiling him in a squabble he did not want, slaying someone other than he intended, or failing to parry a killing blow; armour might cause him to stumble into the path of a *Firestorm* spell. Generally, a Mystic will destroy the item he has made at once if he sees it is flawed. Unfortunately, not all members of the Profession share these scruples.

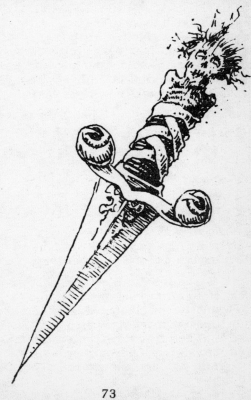

CHAPTER

4 Treasure

Why else would an adventurer choose the hazardous, questing life he leads, if not to acquire treasure? Well, in fact there could be many reasons for a character to go adventuring – vengeance upon an old foe, esteem in the eyes of an adored lady (or lord), the pursuit of glory and excellence in battle, a general desire to confound evil wherever it may lurk. . . These are just a few of the hundreds of possible player-character or NPC motives. That being said, even the most 'verray parfit gentil' Knight would probably admit, however grudgingly, to a certain undercurrent of avarice in his nature.

For the convenience of the GamesMaster, treasure is divided into nine categories of increasing value:

Treasure Type	Cash	Gems/Jewellery	Magic items
Scant	2–20 copper pieces 1–10 silver pieces 0–3 (1d4–1) gold pcs.	none	none
Meagre	3–30 copper 3–30 silver 0–7 gold	0–3 items worth 2–20F each	none
Poor	4–48 silver 1–10 gold	0–5 items worth 50F each	15% chance of 1
Moderate	2–200 silver 2–24 gold	0–7 items worth 10–100F each	30% chance of 1–4
Average	10–1,000 silver 1–100 gold	0–9 items worth 30–300F each	45% chance of 1–6
Good	1,000–10,000 silver 10–1,000 gold	0–11 items worth 100–1,000F each	60% chance of 1–8
Bountiful	2,000–12,000 silver 1,000–8,000 gold	0–19 items worth 1,000–4,000F each	75% chance of 1–10
Grand	5,000–50,000 silver 1,000–20,000 gold	3–30 items worth 1,000–6,000F each	90% chance of 1–12
Fabulous	1,000–100,000 silver 5,000–50,000 gold	5–50 items worth 1,000–8,000F each	1–20

The values quoted for copper, silver and gold may optionally be present in the form of plates, goblets, etc, rather than coins. This obviously makes the treasure more bulky, and generally has the effect of doubling its *encumbrance*.

The monetary system is decimal. (Historians may

take issue with this, but it is the easiest system for game purposes.)

One gold piece, or Crown (1C),
equals ten silver pieces, or Florins (10F),
equals one hundred copper pieces, or Pennies (100P)

Prices are usually given in Florins, except for the most expensive items. Gold is rarely used as currency.

When one or more magic items turn up in treasure, a further roll is needed:

d100	Item
01 – 12	Enchanted armour
13 – 29	Enchanted weapon
30 – 54	Scroll
55 – 79	Potion/Magical compound
80 – 93	Amulet/Talisman
94 – 97	Ring
98 – 00	Unique artifact/relic

Further tables (see Chapter Five) are then used to establish the exact nature of the item.

How is the treasure table used?

The table of treasure types given at the start of this chapter can be used as a GM's guideline when stocking a dungeon or deciding on an appropriate reward for an adventure. Also, creatures of many sorts hoard treasure that they have stolen or scavenged. When creatures are encountered randomly (see **Dragon Warriors 1**, Chapter Eight), they sometimes have treasure – either carried with them, or in their lair or camp nearby:

MONSTERS' TREASURE HOARDS

Monster	Treasure Type (roll d6)
Monster	*Treasure Type (roll d6)*
Apeman	1 – 5 = none; 6 = scant
Basilisk	1 – 2 = moderate; 3 – 6 = average (often petrified)
Bat	none
Bear	none
Bull	none
Crocodile	none
Deaths Head	1 – 4 = moderate; 5 – 6 = average
Dragon	1 = bountiful; 2 – 3 = grand; 4 – 6 = fabulous
Dwarves (in large stronghold)	1 – 2 = good; 3 – 5 = bountiful; 6 = grand
Elemental	none
Elves (in Elf-King's hall	1 – 3 = average; 4 – 5 = good; 6 = bountiful
Gargoyle	1 – 5 = moderate; 6 = average
Frost Giant	1 – 5 = meagre; 6 = poor
Giant Scorpion	none
Ghost	1 – 5 = none; 6 = good
Giant Rat	none
Giant Spider	1 – 4 = none; 5 = poor; 6 = moderate
Gnome	none
Goblin	1 – 3 = meagre; 4 – 6 = poor
Gorgon	1 – 2 = poor; 3 – 5 = moderate; 6 = average
Halflings (in sizable community)	1 – 5 = meagre; 6 = poor
Hobgoblin	1 – 3 = meagre; 4 = poor; 5 = moderate; 6 = average
Horses	none
Humans (in a lord's castle)	1 = average; 2 – 5 = good; 6 = bountiful
Manticore	1 – 5 = none; 6 = average
Ogre	1 – 4 = average; 5 – 6 = good

Obsidiak	none
Orcs	1 – 3 = average; 4 – 6 = good
(in citadel)	
Python	none
Pazuzu	1 – 4 = poor; 5 – 6 = moderate
Snow Ape	none
The Sufiriad	none
Tiger	none
Troll	none
Volucreth	(use NPC Weapons & Equipment table)
Wild Boar	none
Wolf	none
Ghoul	1 – 3 = meagre; 4 – 6 = poor
Mummy	1 – 2 = poor; 3 – 4 = moderate; 5 = average; 6 = good
Skeleton	none
Spectre	none
Wight	1 – 2 = poor; 3 – 5 = moderate; 6 = average
Wraith	none
Zombie	none

Note that the treasures listed for species which live communally – Humans, Elves, Dwarves, Halflings and Orcs – represent the entire hoard of a large community. Volucreths are a special case; adventurers are never likely to encounter an entire society of these belligerent beings!

The treasure possessed by non-player character adventurers is determined using the *NPC Weapons & Equipment* table. Adventurers are unlikely to be found with large amounts of gold and silver. They prefer their wealth in the more useful form of enchanted weaponry and items.

NPC Weapons & Equipment

Non-Player Characters who have adventured may have special items of their own. Because of this, a group of adventurers can be among the most dangerous adversaries that the player-characters are ever likely to face.

When the player-characters encounter a party of NPC adventurers, a table is used to determine whether the latter have special items such as potions and scrolls. The table lists, for each Profession, the chance that the NPC has items of a particular type – and, where applicable, the number of such items that he/she has.

Rank	Profession	Magic Armour	Magic Weapons	Scrolls
1st	Knight	1%	2%; 1	no
	Barbarian	1%	2%; 1	no
	Sorcerer	no	no	1%; 1 – 2
	Mystic	no	no	no
2nd – 3rd	Knight	3%	5%; 1 – 2	no
	Barbarian	2%	5%; 1 – 2	no
	Sorcerer	no	1%; 1	5%; 1 – 4
	Mystic	no	2%; 1	no
4th – 5th	Knight	10%	20%; 1 – 2	no
	Barbarian	8%	20%; 1 – 2	no
	Sorcerer	1%	5%; 1 – 2	25%; 1 – 4
	Mystic	no	20%; 1 – 2	no
6th – 7th	Knight	25%	30%; 1 – 3	no
	Barbarian	15%	30%; 1 – 3	no
	Sorcerer	5%	15%; 1 – 2	40%; 1 – 4
	Mystic	no	30%; 1 – 2	no
8th – 9th	Knight	55%	60%; 1 – 4	no
	Barbarian	40%	60%; 1 – 4	no
	Sorcerer	5%	30%; 1 – 2	50%; 1 – 4
	Mystic	no	70%; 1 – 2	no
10th – up	Knight	80%	90%; 1 – 4	no
	Barbarian	70%	90%; 1 – 4	no
	Sorcerer	5%	40%; 1 – 3	70%; 1 – 6
	Mystic	no	95%; 1 – 3	no

Common sense must be applied to these tables. A Mummy will not be so obliging as to prowl around its tomb with a sack of gold coins over one shoulder. The cash and jewellery component of its treasure may be in a burial chamber some distance from where it is encountered. Hobgoblins can be quite wealthy, but slaying one does not lead to automatic inheritance: the creature's treasure will usually be in its lair, which more often than not is just a narrow clammy burrow deep in the ground.

On the other hand, intelligent creatures will always carry *useful* treasure with them. There is no point in

Potions	Amulets	Rings	Typical cash
3%; 1 – 3	no	no	
1%; 1 – 3	no	no	d100 Florins
30%; 1 – 3	no	no	
2%; 1 – 3	no	no	
15%; 1 – 3	1%; 1 – 2	1%; 1	
15%; 1 – 3	1%; 1 – 2	1%; 1	2d100 Florins
20%; 1 – 4	1%; 1 – 2	2%; 1	
15%; 1 – 3	1%; 1 – 2	2%; 1	
25%; 1 – 3	3%; 1 – 2	3%; 1 – 3	
25%; 1 – 3	3%; 1 – 2	3%; 1 – 3	3d100 Florins
25%; 1 – 4	5%; 1 – 2	5%; 1 – 3	
25%; 1 – 3	4%; 1 – 2	4%; 1 – 3	
35%; 1 – 3	6%; 1 – 2	5%; 1 – 3	
35%; 1 – 3	6%; 1 – 2	5%; 1 – 3	4d100 Florins
50%; 1 – 6	9%; 1 – 2	7%; 1 – 3	
35%; 1 – 3	7%; 1 – 2	7%; 1 – 3	
60%; 1 – 4	10%; 1 – 2	10%; 1 – 3	
60%; 1 – 4	10%; 1 – 2	10%; 1 – 3	4d100 Florins
90%; 1 – 6	10%; 1 – 2	15%; 1 – 3	
60%; 1 – 4	10%; 1 – 2	15%; 1 – 3	
75%; 1 – 4	12%; 1 – 2	10%; 1 – 3	
75%; 1 – 4	12%; 1 – 2	10%; 1 – 3	4d100 Florins
95%; 1 – 4	15%; 1 – 2	15%; 1 – 3	
75%; 1 – 6	12%; 1 – 2	15%; 1 – 3	

owning a +2 sword if it's lying in your treasure chest at home when a bunch of rapacious adventurers jump out at you. There are a few reasons why a creature might not be using a powerful item (eg, it's too holy for the vile monster to touch), but these are the exception.

Trading

Players frequently want to try buying magic items (or conversely, selling items they have and don't need). A few words need to be said about this, for there is actually not much of a market in magic items.

Sorcerers are solitary and do not like being bothered. Additionally, they have little use for money, so even if a Sorcerer of sufficiently high rank can be found he will not necessarily make anything for the player-characters. If he does, he may expect payment in the form of a favour – perhaps a quest he is too old to undertake.

Selling 'spare' items is just as difficult. At first it seems like a good way to make some fast money, but consider the problems. If you are an adventurer with, say, a *Shielding Charm* that you can't use, how are you going to go about selling it? The only people who are likely to want it are other adventurers (a small and elusive part of the populace) or rich nobles (who would probably have one already). The people you offer it to may not be able to muster anything like its real value. And you had better be heavily backed up by your friends, or you might find yourself parting with your precious Charm at knife-point! To summarize, magical merchantry can be a risky business, and is not always especially lucrative – unless you are dealing with folk such as Elves, who really prize any enchanted bauble.

But then, trading with the Elves is an adventure in itself. . .

Magical items fall into these groups:

> Enchanted armour and weapons
> Scrolls
> Potions and magical compounds
> Talismans and amulets
> Rings
> Unique artifacts and relics

Earlier sections (Chapter Two and Three) have already described how these items can be created by Sorcerers and Mystics, given time. But adventurers tend to be impatient people. They rarely wish to devote months or painstaking years to constructing a magical device, and much prefer to acquire these things in the form of plundered treasure.

ENCHANTED ARMOUR

Any item of magical armour has a magic bonus: + 1, + 2 or + 3. This indicates how magical it is. The magic bonus is added on to the regular Armour Factor. + 2 ring mail thus has an AF of 5.

For any item found in treasure, two rolls must be made. First to determine the armour type:

d100	Armour
01 – 10	Hardened leather
11 – 50	Ring mail
51 – 70	Chainmail
71 – 00	Plate

and then to find out its magical bonus:

d100	Magic bonus
01 – 55	+ 1
56 – 85	+ 2
86 – 00	+ 3

ENCHANTED WEAPONS

Magical weapons also have a magic bonus. In the case of a normal melee weapon, the bonus is added to the user's ATTACK, DEFENCE, Armour Bypass Rolls and to the damage inflicted on a successful hit. Using the notation of DRAGON WARRIORS 1, a normal sword is a (d8, 4 points) weapon. Enchanted to + 2, the same sword becomes a (d8 + 2, 6 points) weapon – and its owner gains 2 ATTACK and 2 DEFENCE points while fighting with it.

In the case of a missile weapon such as an arrow, the magic bonus is added to the user's ATTACK, Armour Bypass Roll and (if the arrow strikes home) to the wound it inflicts.

Where shields are concerned, the magic bonus is added to the user's DEFENCE.

As with armour, two rolls are made:

d100	Weapon
01 – 10	Arrows (quiver of six)
11 – 20	Battleaxe
21 – 30	Dagger
31 – 40	Morning Star
41 – 45	Quarrels (case of ten)
46 – 55	Shortsword

56 – 60	Spear
61 – 80	Sword
81 – 85	Two-handed Sword
86 – 95	Shield
96 – 00	Other (Halberd, Javelin, etc)

And, for the degree of enchantment:

d100	*Magic bonus*
01 – 45	+ 1
46 – 80	+ 2
81 – 00	+ 3

There is a chance that any enchanted item may be flawed. This applies to armour as well as weapons. The chance is very small – most flawed items are destroyed by the Mystic who forged them, and many of the remainder are shunned as their baneful powers become known. The chance that an enchanted item is flawed is 3% for a + 1 item, 2% for a + 2 and 1% for a + 3. Mystics may be able to detect the flaw in such an item using their Sixth Sense. If they do not, and a character uses the item, disaster is inevitable. (See Chapter Three, ENCHANTMENT OF ARMS & ARMOUR.)

SCROLLS

Scrolls are illuminated parchments on which a spell is written. By reading the spell aloud, a Sorcerer (not necessarily the Sorcerer who wrote it) casts the spell – but he expends no *Magic Points*, because the energy for the spell was invested in the scroll when it was written. Once the scroll is used, it disintegrates. Scrolls are one-use items.

Scrolls may be of spells up to the ninth level. Scrolls of first and second level are almost never found because there is no advantage to be gained in inscribing them – each scroll written out reduces the calligrapher's *Magic Point* score by 2 until it is used.

A d100 roll determines the level of the spell written on any scroll found as treasure:

d100	Level of spell
01 – 10	third
11 – 30	fourth
31 – 55	fifth
56 – 75	sixth
76 – 90	seventh
91 – 96	eighth
97 – 00	ninth

Then roll randomly (ie, d6) to find the specific spell within the level. Spells which can have a variable number of *Magic Points* in them will usually have the minimum necessary to cast the spell (eg, 4 *MPs* for a *Wall of Magic*).

If the dice rolls indicate a *Rune*, the scroll is actually booby-trapped. Instead of being a scroll of the *Rune* spell, it is a piece of parchment with a *Rune* inscribed on it. The *Rune* will discharge the spell it contains (generally something along the lines of *Deathlight* or *Stasis*) as soon as it is unfurled.

A Sorcerer who has found a scroll does not have to use it in order to find out what spell it is. He will recognize any spell that he *knows* – that is not of a higher level than his rank – by looking at it. Only when he reads the scroll *aloud* is the spell cast. Inability to recognize the spell does not prevent him from reciting it to find out what it does. If Gothique (a 1st rank Sorcerer we met earlier) found a *Firestorm* scroll he would not have a clue what it did, but he could still read it aloud and so cast the spell.

POTIONS AND MAGICAL COMPOUNDS

Potions found in treasure will normally be in a flask containing one dose. There is a 20% chance that the potion was incorrectly prepared. Usually this means that it will simply not work, but in a very few cases (whenever the GamesMaster feels like having some fun) there will be some unexpected effect. (So a misbrewed Potion of Occult Acuity might actually take away the drinker's spellcasting ability for a time. Healing Potion might inflict a wound, etc.)

There will not always be a label on the bottle to say what the potion is; even if there is a label, it might be wrong. A Sorcerer will recognize any potion once he has prepared it in the laboratory, from distinctive odours and colour. Other than this, the surest way to tell what a potion does is to drink it!

For each potion found, the GM rolls d100:

d100 roll	Potion
01 – 12	Potion of Dexterity
13 – 22	Potion of Occult Acuity
23 – 34	Potion of Strength
35 – 42	Healing Potion
43 – 46	Replenishment Potion
47 – 48	Amianthus Dust
49 – 60	Potion of Night Vision
61 – 62	Dust of Transformation
63 – 64	Elixir Vitae
65 – 66	Evaporating Potion
67 – 68	Sands of Slumber
69 – 76	Vial of Smoke
77 – 78	Aitheron
79 – 80	Hydon
81 – 82	Lithon
83 – 84	Phlogiston
85 – 86	Potion of Dreams
87 – 89	Theriac
90 – 92	Poison
93 – 94	Potion of Control
95 – 96	Love Philtre
97 – 98	Potion of Truth
99 – 00	Virus Lunare

The effects of these various concoctions are as follows:

Potion of Dexterity

Drinking this potion will raise the character's *Reflexes* score by 4 points, up to a maximum score of 18. This enables the character to act earlier than he would normally in a Combat Round and may increase his ATTACK, DEFENCE and EVASION scores. The effect is of course only temporary; a Spell Expiry Roll is applied to determine its duration.

Potion of Occult Acuity

This adds 4 points to the drinker's *Psychic Talent* score, up to a maximum of 18. This may increase his MAGICAL ATTACK (if any) and MAGICAL DEFENCE scores. A Spell Expiry Roll indicates when the effect wears off.

Potion of Strength

This enhances the character's *Strength* by 4 points, up to a maximum of 20. His ATTACK and DEFENCE scores will be affected and also, possibly, his Armour Bypass Rolls and melee weapon damage. Again, a Spell Expiry Roll sets the duration.

Healing Potion

This potion has a curative effect on any wounds the drinker has sustained. One full draught is equivalent to a spell of *Greater Healing*, but it is also possible to obtain some benefit from only half a dose (treat as a *Lesser Healing*).

Replenishment Potion

When a Sorcerer drinks this potion he recovers 2 – 8 (roll 2d4) expended *Magic Points*. It will not take him above his normal *MP* limit. When drunk by a Mystic, the potion allows him to subtract 1 from his next Psychic Fatigue Check die roll (if he is not already psychically fatigued) or give him the ability to cast one 'free' spell of up to fourth level (if he is).

Amianthus Dust

Sprinkling this heavy black powder over a character will give him limited protection from the effects of flame and excessive heat. He becomes completely immune to normal fire and takes only half damage from supernatural fire (a Dragon's breath, a *Firestorm* spell, etc). A Spell Expiry Roll indicates when the effect wears off.

Potion of Night Vision

Quaffing this blue-black fluid gives the ability to see in the darkness of night as though it were day. The utter blackness of a dungeon will seem like twilight. The effect lasts for two hours.

Dust of Transformation

This must be hurled to the ground at a character's feet. In a puff of smoke and a dazzling flash he will be metamorphosed into another form. This is like the *Transformation* spell, except that a Spell Expiry Roll applies. The form is predetermined when the ingredients are mixed and so, unless the container is labelled, the usefulness of the dust can only be established by trial –

the user might find himself turned into a morose toad!
The most common forms 'encoded' into Dust of Transformation are Wolves, Bears, Pythons, Tigers, Bats
and Giant Spiders. Gorgons are also favoured: the
transformed character does not really acquire 'the
eyes that fossilize' – but any enemy who mistakes him
for a real Gorgon won't know that! If the character
wishes to resist being changed by the dust's power, he
must roll d20 and score less than or equal to his
MAGICAL DEFENCE.

Elixir Vitae

A prized potion. Poured between the lips of a corpse, it
has the effect of restoring life. The revitalized character loses 1d3 *Health Points* and 1 point from each of his
characteristics (*Strength*, etc) permanently. The
potion may not work properly if the character has been
dead for more than a month; there is then a 50%
chance that he will be raised as a horrible Ghoul
instead of a living man. After a year and a day, the
Elixir has no chance of working.

Evaporating Potion

Moments after imbibing this rancid brew, a character
will dissolve into a dank sulphurous mist. This is no bad
thing, however, for in 'mist form' the character is able
to drift slowly along at 3m per Combat Round. This
means that he can seep under doors or through tiny
cracks. Another advantage is that the character will
not take damage from nonmagical weapons or indirect-
attack spells. A Spell Expiry Roll determines when the
character returns to his normal form. A character who
wishes to resist the potion's subliming effect can do so
by rolling less than or equal to his MAGICAL DEFENCE
on d20.

Sands of Slumber

This compound is usually tied up in a flimsy pouch which can be flung at an intended victim. It is then treated as a normal hand-hurled missile. The pouch splits when it strikes the target, scattering the abrasive dust over him. It is also possible to fling a loose handful directly into his face, but this can only be done at point-blank range and is not feasible if the target is weaving about in melee. The target character must, if hit by the dust, roll less than or equal to his *Reflexes* to avoid getting the Sands of Slumber in his eyes. If he fails this roll he becomes drowsy (treat as a *Weaken* spell) and will lapse inexorably into a deep sleep within 2 – 8 Combat Rounds. The character can only be aroused from this dreamless repose if another approaches him with honest intent to kill him. If this happens he will awaken at once, but otherwise he will sleep for a hundred years.

Vial of Smoke

This volatile mixture is usually stored in a fragile clay bottle or tube of crystal. When the container is smashed, a dense cloud of white fog forms rapidly, billowing out to a distance of 5m. Visibility is nil, even for a character using *Clairvoyance*. A d6 is rolled at the start of each subsequent Combat Round; on a roll of '6', the fog disperses.

The Elemental Essences

These potions summon or create an Elemental, which may then serve the user for a time. Each looks quite different – Aitheron, which materializes an Air Elemental, is a thick resinous substance which must be scattered into the air. When poured into water, Hydon creates a Water Elemental. Lithon is a moist chalky deposit which, mixed with soil or pebbles, causes an Earth Elemental to appear. Phlogiston bursts alight at the merest spark and a Fire Elemental will coalesce from the flames. The character must make a special roll to see if he commands the Elemental: his rank or less on d12. A failed roll means that the Elemental is free to enjoy an orgy of destruction, which will usually begin with its summoner. The Elemental will fade after half an hour, unless slain before that.

Potion of Dreams

This must be imbibed before going to sleep, causing the drinker to experience visions of events past, present and future. The intention is to glean something of direct bearing on the drinker, but the potion is unreliable and may reveal a pageant of irrelevant fantasies. Nothing is what is seems to be in the murky realm of the subconscious. Events may appear in symbolic form; the GM just informs the player what he has dreamed, and leaves the latter to interpret it for himself.

Theriac

This is a universal antidote which will neutralize any poison in the character's bloodstream. It does not heal any physical damage (lost *Health Points*) already inflicted by the poison.

Poison

This covers, as they say, a multitude of sins. The ingredients cost given earlier is for a normal strength poison (roll *Strength* or less on 3d6 or die). Weak (2d6) poison costs half as much to make. Strong poison costs double.

It is also possible to concoct 'fancy' poisons – things that only paralyse, weaken, impair reflexes, etc, if the required roll is not made. Most poisons are made to be administered orally, but that is not the only kind. Some Sorcerers make venoms that can be smeared onto a blade or arrow-point. Exposure to air renders the venom inactive if the weapon is not then used within one minute (10 Combat Rounds).

Potion of Control

The character must trick his intended victim into drinking this potion – perhaps by claiming that it is some beneficial substance such as a Healing Potion. The drinker will obey the first person who gives him an order. This control lasts for a full day. It can be terminated prematurely with a *Dispel Magic* cast with at least 9 *Magic Points*, and wears off automatically if the controlled character is ordered to kill himself or a loved one.

Love Philtre

This is another potion that the victim must be tricked into imbibing. Unfortunately, unlike Potion of Control, it is completely tasteless and can be mixed with food or drink. The drinker falls in love with the first character of the opposite sex whom he lays eyes on after taking the philtre. This can only be broken by keeping the afflicted character from his beloved for at least a year. Force will probably be necessary.

Potion of Truth

The character who drinks this bright golden liquid must give a truthful answer to any question that is put to him during the three minutes that follow.

Virus Lunare

This is an obscene brew which no decent Sorcerer would ever dream of preparing. Unfortunately, it must be said that a sizable minority of Sorcerers are hopelessly vile. They make this leprous distillation between nights of the full moon. It must be administered to a person whom the Sorcerer must then slay with his own hands. The potion traps a tortured fragment of the victim's soul within the shell of his corpse; and when the Sorcerer casts *Reanimate the Dead* upon the body it will arise as a Zombie, bound in unending service to him until a second 'death' might give it surcease.

AMULETS & TALISMANS

The words amulet and talisman tend to be used interchangeably nowadays. Both are magical devices worn around the neck. If there is any functional distinction to be drawn it is that talismans (the first six on the list below) bestow some continual advantage on the user, whereas the powers of amulets (the last six items on the list) are restricted in frequency or duration.

d100	Talisman/Amulet
01–05	Periapt
06–12	Blue Scarab
13–30	Abraxus Stone
31–35	Auric Pendulum
36–50	Eye of Foreboding
51–60	Stone of Valiance
61–65	Ankh of Osiris
66–75	Shielding Charm
76–85	Amulet of Sovereignty over Violence
86–89	Key to the Dark Labyrinth
90–96	Pendant of Alarums
97–00	Amulet of Soul Storing

Only one amulet or talisman can be employed by a character at any given time. If he tries to wear more, their powers will interfere with one another and he will be unable to make them work.

The powers of these items are as follows.

The Periapt

This is a simple stone with a hole through it, usually mounted on a leather thong. Worn about the neck, it affords some protection against Curses and possession (eg, by the spirit in an Amulet of Soul Storing). The wearer gets a + 4 bonus to MAGICAL DEFENCE where such attacks are concerned.

The Blue Scarab

This talisman, in the shape of a faience beetle on a silver chain, defends the wearer against poison and disease. Whenever he is exposed to any disease (natural or sorcerous) or toxin, d100 is rolled. On a roll of 01 – 15, the attack is completely neutralized.

The Abraxus Stone

This enhances the wearer's recuperative powers. His rate of natural recovery from wounds is speeded by an additional 1 *Health Point* per day. This applies only to wounds he took while wearing the talisman. This item is an oval of polished white onyx incised with a red glyph.

The Auric Pendulum

This consists of a bob of grey marble hanging on a copper rod. When brought within 15m of a large quantity of gold (at least 500 Crowns or an equivalent weight), the Auric Pendulum swings towards it.

The Eye of Foreboding

This is a small globe of rose quartz which glows faintly when anything tries to sneak up on the wearer with evil intent. The warning glow is imperceptible in daylight, but below ground in dungeons, caverns, etc, it will prevent its wearer from being *surprised* (see **Dragon Warriors 1**, Chapter Six, *Encounters*).

The Stone of Valiance

This talisman, a small sapphire with a triangle engraved upon it, is said to make its wearer fearless. Any *fright attack* against him, whether due to ghostly manifestation or malevolent sorcery, is halved in strength.

The Ankh of Osiris

Once donned, this amulet cannot be removed until its power has been used. It will restore the wearer to life if he or she is killed. This revivification is immediate and, apart from the permanent loss of 1 *Health Point*, ensures full vitality. Having performed its function, the amulet loses all magical power.

The Shielding Charm

This amulet takes the form of a silver pentagram on a small tablet of oak. When commanded by the wearer to protect him, the amulet produces a tiny black point in the air, around which images appear shimmering and distorted as above a fire. The effect is accompanied by a faint droning sound. The hovering black dot moves rapidly to intercept any fast-moving object that is about to strike the wearer. The wearer rolls d6 for each blow that would otherwise hit him; on a roll of

4 – 6, the blow is deflected. A Spell Expiry Roll is used to determine how long the effect lasts. The amulet will operate twice in one day, recovering its powers at midnight.

The Amulet of Sovereignty over Violence

A sparkling diamond on a white gold chain, this amulet imbues the wearer's body with supernatural toughness. Any wounds he takes are halved (round fractions up.) A normal sword would thus inflict only a 2 *HP* wound instead of the usual 4 *HP*. The duration of this effect is set by a Spell Expiry Roll. This amulet operates once per day; once used, its powers regenerate at midnight.

The Key of the Dark Labyrinth

A talmi-gold key wound with lacquered strands of human, this amulet is particularly bizarre in its effect. Any being who wounds the wearer in melee while the amulet is in use experiences a sorcerous attack. The effect has a MAGICAL ATTACK of 20, matched against the being's MAGICAL DEFENCE just like a spell. If the attack works, the being disappears from this world and is transported to a confusing other-dimensional maze. The being must find his/its way through this maze in order to return to the real world; 2d4 are rolled every Combat Round, and on a roll of 8 he/it reappears. A Spell Expiry Roll applies to the effect of this amulet, and once it is used it will not function again that day.

(*Special note*: There may come a time when a player-character attacks someone using this amulet and suffers its effect. Rather than have him make the 2d4 rolls to abstractly represent his plight, you could actually map out a simple maze and see how long he takes to get through it.)

The Pendant of Alarums

This is a small steel bar on a steel chain. It enables the wearer to set invisible alarm-spells on the back of doors, the lid of a chest, floors, windows, etc. When any being passes that way, the amulet produces a soft chime. To receive the alarm, the owner of the amulet must be within 250m and wearing his amulet at the time. Up to nine different alarm-spells can be set with the amulet, and the warning from each alarm-spell has its own characteristic pitch. (A problem: Is the wearer tone-deaf?) If the wearer removes the amulet, any alarm-spells he has set are negated. An alarm-spell is also negated when it is tripped.

The Amulet of Soul Storing

This can be made to look like any one of the preceding amulets and talismans. Its function is to contain the wearer's soul if he is slain. If another person then puts on the amulet, the soul can attempt to possess him. This is resolved like a direct-attack spell, matching the MAGICAL ATTACK that the dead character had in life against the MAGICAL DEFENCE of the victim. (If the character did not have a MAGICAL ATTACK score, his soul attacks with an effective MAGICAL ATTACK of 2d6 + his MAGICAL DEFENCE.) Even if the first attempt at possession fails, the soul can try again and again (once each Combat Round) until the amulet is removed. Successful possession means that the soul takes up residence in the victim's body (acquiring the appearance, *Strength* and *Reflexes* of the host but retaining the skills and memories of its original self) while the victim's soul is displaced into the amulet. (Such an amulet found in treasure will often − 80% of the time − have a soul trapped within it. Roll 3d4 to find the soul's rank when alive and d4 for its Profession; this yields the appropriate MAGICAL ATTACK with which to assail whichever unsuspecting player-character puts the amulet on.)

RINGS

Any character with a *Psychic Talent* score of at least 9 can use magic rings. Rings must be worn on the left hand, and wearing more than three at a time will prevent any of them from functioning. Activating a ring is an action, taking one Combat Round. Those rings which have charges will be found with 3d8 – 3; they can be recharged up to the maximum capacity of 21 charges by any Sorcerer of 8th rank or higher. The time required for this is one lunar month per charge.

One problem with rings is finding out what they do. There are hundreds of different forms a ring might take: a plain silver band, a coiled serpent in bronze, an amythest in a gold setting, an intricate filigree. . . Whatever the maker chose, in fact. Appearance is no clue to function. Only a few (perhaps one in ten) bear any inscription, so often the only way to find out what the ring is is to try it out.

Rings found in treasure:

d100	Type
01 – 20	Ring of Agonizing Doom
21 – 27	Ring of the Burning Halo
28 – 34	Ring of Negation
35 – 40	Ring of Obedient Parts
41 – 45	Ring of Psychic Chains
46 – 66	Ring of Red Ruin
67 – 87	Ring of Sentinels
88 – 00	Ring of Teleportation

The Ring of Agonizing Doom

Each charge of this ring generates a bolt of emerald lightning which forks out towards the nearest 2 – 8 beings in the direction the ringwearer is pointing. The bolt has a SPEED of 12 and a maximum range of 20m. Each being struck takes 2d8 *HP* damage, reduced by his/its Armour Factor if any.

The Ring of the Burning Halo

This surrounds the user with a coruscating circle of white fire $2\frac{1}{2}$m in radius. Any being attempting to cross this halo will take 2d6 *Health Points* damage; again, armour (or tough skin/scales) protects by absorbing its AF from this damage. Each use of the ring costs one charge and lasts until terminated by a Spell Expiry Roll.

The Ring of Negation

A charge of this ring produces a glittering beam of anti-magical energy. This beam can be directed at a single durational spell within its range of 10m. If the spell was cast with 8 *Magic Points* or less (Mystic spells: cast at eighth level or less) it is dispelled at once.

The Ring of Obedient Parts

When this ring is constructed, an outre entity of unguessable origin and nature is somehow summoned and trapped within it. Upon command, the entity within the ring will release one of its constituent sections. A large yellow eye, hand or mouth appears in the air and waits for the ringwearer's telepathic orders. These parts can float through the air at 10m per Combat Round (six kilometres an hour, a brisk walking pace) and are prepared to go any distance to serve their master. The eye can record visual images and play them back, in the form of a monochrome projection on any suitable surface, when it returns to its master. The hand can fetch and carry anything that a man could lift with one arm. It can sense objects around it, but cannot 'see' clearly and thus is unable to wield a sword. The lips will carry messages and return to tell their master what they have heard – unlike the other two forms, the lips have an acoustic sense; like the hand, they 'see' only hazy shapes. All three forms hover at a height of no more than 5m above the ground. When one form has returned to the ring, the entity within can be made to send forth another. There is no restriction on the duration or number of uses of this ring, but only one of the three parts can be manifest at any given time.

The Ring of Psychic Chains

Sucker bait left around by sneaky Sorcerers. This ring negates a Sorcerer's or Mystic's ability to use spells the moment he slips it on to his finger. Mere force is insufficient to remove the ring – this must be accomplished with an 8 *Magic Point* spell of *Dispel Magic* or, more drastically, by severing the finger.

The Ring of Red Ruin

At the cost of one charge, this ring emits a beam of searing light towards a single target within 20m. If the target fails to dodge (the beam has a SPEED of 20), he suffers 1d20 *HP* damage. Magical armour will reduce the damage taken by its magic bonus; nonmagical armour is ineffective.

The Ring of Sentinels

With each charge expended, the wearer can bring an unhuman Knight from another world to fight for him. These Sentinels have blue-white skin, violet eyes that pierce even the total dark of an underworld, and wear gilded armour of quite unearthly design. The stats of a Sentinel are:

ATTACK 16   Two-handed sword (d10, 5 points)
DEFENCE 10   Armour Factor 4
MAGICAL DEFENCE 6   Movement: 10m/
EVASION 4   Combat Round
Health Points 1d6 + 10   Rank-equivalent: 4th

For each Sentinel summoned, a Spell Expiry Roll is used to determine how long it remains on this Plane. The ringwearer can summon no more than three Sentinels at a time — he must then wait until one of them is slain or vanishes of its own accord before he can use the ring again.

The Ring of Teleportation

This enables the ringwearer to teleport up to 150m instantaneously. He must have some familiarity with his intended destination to be sure of arriving safely. A place counts as 'familiar' in this context if the wearer has studied it first-hand for at least five minutes in the past hour, or ten minutes in the past two hours, and so on. Any place he has carefully scrutinized for over thirty minutes on two separate occasions counts as permanently familiar; he can teleport to it in perfect safety at any time he is within range. If he teleports without taking these precautions, to a location he hardly knows, roll d100. There is a 70% chance the teleport will work properly, a 25% chance that it will be to some random location within 150m, and a 5% chance that the ring will turn the wearer inside out and back to front before ejecting him into another dimensional continuum where he is lost forever! It is possible to use the Ring of Teleportation to transport someone else; the wearer must physically touch the character he is trying to teleport, and the latter may wish to resist the effect (match the ring's MAGICAL ATTACK of 20 vs the character's MAGICAL DEFENCE). Each use of the ring, whether to teleport the wearer or another character, uses up one charge.

ARTIFACTS

Magical artifacts are usually unique. Most are the fruit of a lifetime (or more) of work by a dedicated (or crazy) magician. Player characters who attain very high rank (15th or more) could attempt to devise artifacts of their own. Powerful magic, unlike modern science, is not always reproducible; artifacts constructed by two different Sorcerers will always differ in some way, even if they have the same general effect.

Some of the artifacts which could feature in a campaign are given below. GamesMasters should devise their own additions to this list – partly so that the artifacts reflect the mood and setting of the campaign, and partly so that players cannot cheat and find out what a unique item does by looking it up in this book!

Felgor's Visor

The warlord Felgor (called 'the Reaver') possessed a helmet with a visor of blue-grey metal fashioned into the aspect of a terrible demon. The character who wears this helmet can cause it to discharge a bolt of raging energy to a distance of 10m. The bolt has a SPEED of 12. Use of this power drains energy from the wearer – for each *Health Point* he expends, the bolt inflicts 1d4 *HP* damage on the victim (who subtracts his Armour Factor from the total damage rolled).

The Tempest Horn

When this horn is blown, a wind arises from nowhere. Within a minute (10 Combat Rounds), storm clouds will have covered the sky and a localized tempest, 150m across, will rage around the horn's user. Within the storm zone, rain driven by the fierce gale reduces visibility to 5m, and the continuous rumble of thunder and shrieking winds make normal communication impossible. Beings caught in the storm move at half their normal rate, and flying characters/creatures have a 10% chance each Round of being dashed from the sky. There is also a 5% chance every Combat Round that a bolt of fork lightning will strike 2 – 12 beings in the storm zone, inflicting 6d6 *HP* damage (the victim can subtract his AF if he is wearing *magic* armour). At the very centre of the zone is an area of calm, the eye of the storm, 3m across; thus, the user of the horn remains safe from danger. The storm lasts ten minutes and then dies as suddenly as it appeared. The horn is evidently usable only outside, and but once per week.

The Sword of Darkness

This thin blade of black metal is said in some folktales to have been forged by the Devil himself, and most warriors would be loath to use it in spite of its magic. It confers no bonuses to the wielder's Combat Factors, but uses a 20-sided dice for Armour Bypass Rolls and inflicts a 5 *HP* wound. The sword has a certain sentience (reputedly evil) of its own. It can make its wishes and feelings known to its owner by empathy, and has three spells which it can use once a day: *Shadowbolt*, *Mantlet* and *Nova*. It casts these at its own whim, not necessarily when its owner needs them.

The Crown of Truth

Whoever wears this unadorned circlet of gold has a 75% chance of seeing through any illusion at first glance. Simply touching the illusion will cause it to vanish.

St. Goldmund's Locker

This is a wooden casket of moderate size, bound with bands of iron. It counts as 'two items' for encumbrance purposes; but in fact up to fifteen items, each as big as a man, can be fitted within! Placing an item in the locker takes one Combat Round; removing an item takes two Combat Rounds.

The Torc of Continual Restoration

This very powerful magical item continually regenerates the body of the character who wears it. He or she heals at the rate of 1 *Health Point* per Combat Round. Lost limbs or organs will grow back within an hour, and even if the character is killed he will rise from the dead once the Torc restores him to positive *Health Points*. The only type of wound not restored by the Torc is that caused by fire – including natural flame, spells of *Dragonbreath*, *Nova* or *Firestorm*, the breath of a Dragon, etc. Once fixed around a character's neck, the Torc will clamp shut; it can only be removed when the character is dead.

Flying Carpets

A number of famous wizards created flying carpets. The great Sorcerer Norfengu even built a flying palanquin! The exact powers of various flying carpets differ, but most will bear a load of four or five people at speeds of up to 75 km/hour. To operate a flying carpet one must know the command words to make it *come, land, take off, fly straight on, turn left, turn right, gain altitude, lose altitude*. Sometimes the last two commands are subsumed into the *land/take-off* commands. Sometimes the carpet will have a wider range of commands. Aktrium the Mage made his flying carpet respond to the tunes he played on a flute, but was undone when a Hobgoblin piper mimicked his notes. To gain maximum manoeuvrability, the renowned Ranulf Deathgaze created a flying throne that responded to his thoughts, though with the drawback that he needed full concentration to operate the device and could not cast spells while in flight.

The Sceptre of the North

This is a short rod of silvery metal with a glyph-incised sphere at one end. Pressing a catch on the side releases a tremendous bolt of force that will demolish stout doors, blast 20cm into solid rock, or deal 4d10 *HP* damage to a being who fails to evade it (SPEED 14). The beam is quite narrow, so it will strike only a single person, and the range is 5m. The Sceptre operates three times and then takes 48 hours to recharge itself. This device was invented by the Companions of the Ice, reclusive priests of the nemesis-god Angaril, and it is rumoured that they constructed at least ten such sceptres to further their nefarious goals.

Orric's Slates

Though well-versed in powerful sorcery, Orric was a gentle priest who loved scholasticism. He made two slates with the property that whatever is written on one will appear at the same time on the other, regardless of the distance between them. (Characters may, of course, come across one without the other – unkind GMs, take note!)

The Mirror of the Moon

The owner of this strange device can cause it to create a soulless, nearly mindless simulacrum of a single opponent within 5m. The simulacrum has the fighting skills and other characteristics of the person it resembles – and also has duplicates of his arms and armour, though it has not the wit to use any magical devices he happens to possess. It will attack its original to the exclusion of all else – using only physical attacks, for it can neither use magic nor be affected by it. Once it has slain the original, it fades from existence. If the original defeats the simulacrum, the Mirror shatters; otherwise, it can be used once a week.

The Cloak of Invisibility

Whenever this dark red cloak is donned, the wearer becomes invisible to the eyes of any character below 6th rank. However, the wearer must exert some concentration for the Cloak to work properly. If his concentration is broken (for instance, if he is wounded, or wishes to attack, or cast a spell) he appears as a flickering shadowy form to characters of 1st to 5th rank, though he retains full invisibility where normal mortals (ie, unranked characters not belonging to an adventuring Profession) are concerned.

Wristband of Extreme Luck

This faceted jade vambrace enhances the wearer's luck in dire emergencies. In game-terms, its powers apply whenever a dice roll is being made and only one specific number will be of benefit to the wearer. In these cases, 1 is added to or subtracted from the roll, as needed. For example, if the wearer were trying to strike an opponent whose DEFENCE is higher than his own ATTACK, he would normally hit only on a '1' on d20. The Wristband subtracts 1 from the die roll, meaning that he hits on a 1 or a 2.

RELICS

A relic is a tooth, bone, lock of hair, or other fragment of a saint's mortal remains. Such fragments may be stored within a *reliquary* — often a crucifix or sword-pommel — and have power against unholy beings.

The exact powers of relics vary. All give the owner some chance of sensing great evil when it is present in an object, place or person. Other powers should ideally be at the discretion of the GamesMaster, who may or may not wish to follow these guidelines:

First roll d10 for the *quality* of the relic:

d10	quality	powers
1 – 2	holy	10% chance of sensing evil; one additional power – roll 2d6 – 1 and consult the list below.
3 – 7	saintly	20% chance of sensing evil; two additional powers – roll 2d6 for each on table below.
8 – 9	perfect	40% chance of sensing evil; three additional powers – roll 2d6 + 1 for each on table below.
0	godly	80% chance of sensing evil; three additional powers – roll 2d6 + 3 for each on table below.

Then roll for *additional powers* as indicated:

dice roll	power
1	+ 1 DEFENCE when fighting Goblins, Hobgoblins or Trolls
2	+ 1 MAGICAL DEFENCE vs Hobgoblin sorcery
3	+ 1 DEFENCE when fighting Undead
4	+ 1 ATTACK when fighting Goblins, Hobgoblins or Trolls
5	+ 1 ATTACK when fighting Undead
6	+ 1 MAGICAL DEFENCE vs Elven magic
7	+ 1 MAGICAL DEFENCE vs Undead magic
8	+ 1 MAGICAL DEFENCE vs all sorcery
9	+ 2 DEFENCE vs Undead, Goblins, Hobgoblins & Trolls
10	+ 2 ATTACK vs Undead, Goblins, Hobgoblins & Trolls
11	+ 2 MAGICAL DEFENCE vs Undead and Hobgoblin magic
12	immunity to fright attack and Vampire mesmerism

13	power to exorcize Ghosts
14	inflict twice normal damage in combat with Undead
15	power to drive away Undead (takes three Combat Rounds)

GamesMasters may wish to restrict the use of relics to devout characters. Sorcerers are not evil, but the power they use is intrinsically pagan and they are consequently unable to benefit from a relic.

Abbeys prize these items because ownership of a relic confers status on an abbey. If a relic is taken to the monks then they may pay well for it. However, if they see any excuse for deeming the owner unworthy (and if he is not of too high rank!), they will simply confiscate the relic and throw the character out!

The following scenarios, *A Shadow On The Mist* and *Hunter's Moon*, are intended for a party of about four characters of 1st – 3rd rank.

A SHADOW ON THE MIST

General note:

A short scenario, best suited to a party with a high proportion of Sorcerers and Mystics.

Overview of the adventure:

The characters are summoned to the manor house of the village in which they're staying. They meet Sir Beorn, steward of the local lord, who dispatches them on a mission to a strange, shunned, fog-shrouded hollow. This is the abode of an evil Wight, twisted revenant of the high king buried here in ancient times. The characters must enter the mists of the hollow and return with the items Beorn needs.

GM: Throughout the scenario, sections which may be paraphrased or read out wholesale to the players are

in italics. Other sections concern monster statistics, unobvious or hidden details, and other information; these are for your eyes only.

I. The adventure begins

It is dawn. As the sun rises over the fields around Axbridge, you are already out on the village green, exercising and practicing your combat drill. You are surprised to see Notker, a short ruddy-cheeked fellow who serves as the lord's bailiff, running along the street towards you. He stops for a few moments to catch his breath, then calls out, "Come with me to the manor. Sir Beorn, steward to the baron, is here. He wishes to speak with you!"

GM: A brief word about the social order is perhaps appropriate here. The estates of the baron, whose castle lies several days' ride to the east, are widely scattered. He cannot personally supervise them all, so he has a steward to take care of this. Sir Beorn spends much of his time overseeing the various villages of the fief. In his absence, responsibility for the manor house resides with the bailiff, who is himself of peasant stock.

Most of the villagers would be suspicious of adventurers – though they are always ready to feed and shelter anyone who pays good money. The bailiff, Notker, would rarely speak to them; he is an honest and pious man who distrusts those who live by their wits. For the steward, a gruff old Knight and veteran of the Crusades, to summon common adventurers into the manor house is truly remarkable. The players should realize that something of great importance must be in the offing.

Notker ushers you into the long hall of the manor house. The steward, Beorn, waits impatiently. He is a broad-shouldered man with a fierce stern face, and he wastes no time on pleasantries.

"Up in hills by Norham Wood there is a hollow that the locals call Hob's Dell. They believe it to be a magic place, and won't go near it. I need some people who aren't afraid of churls' fireside tales." He hurls a fat bag of coins down onto the table. *"A hundred and fifty silver Florins. You get fifty now, and the rest after you've done the job. There may be treasure along the way, and you can keep one tenth of any that you find. Interested?"*

GM: Beorn is most definitely not a man to haggle. If the characters try to strike a better bargain, he will curtly motion them to leave. If they change their minds then, they will find the fee has dropped by thirty Florins!

Assuming that they accept, Beorn goes on to explain:

"The baron's tax collector passed through Norham from here two days ago, heading for the castle. He had the taxes of four manors in his saddlebags. A few hours later, his horse limped back into Norham without him. The taxes were missing also, and a fine sword I was sending as a gift for my brother. The horse must have thrown him up by Norham Wood — perhaps a Goblin frightened it, pah! His neck can be broken for all I care, but I want that sword back. And if the taxes aren't recovered, the peasants will have to pay twice this year. Not a pleasant thought, with winter coming on."

His scowl tells you it is not the peasants' welfare that concerns him.

GM: Much of what Beorn has told them is true, but he has omitted some salient details. As the characters leave, they may begin to see holes in Beorn's story. Why does he assume the tax collector was up near Hob's Dell? Why is he so anxious to recover the lost

114

sword? (Naturally, they are asking for trouble if they make any such doubts known to Beorn!)

The facts. Beorn and two of his men met up with the tax collector (whose name was Harald) a few days ago, in the small village of Hesard's Ford. Beorn gave him the sword and asked him to deliver it into the hand of Beorn's brother when he reached the castle. In fact, the sword itself was of no importance – but concealed within its pommel was a message from Beorn which incriminates him in a plot on the baron's life. Harald heard Beorn talking with his men, realized what was afoot, and departed at once. They soon discovered his absence and set out in pursuit – Beorn coming west to Axbridge while his men covered the northern road.

Harald was indeed heading north, and the men caught up with him just beyond Norham. He fled from the road up into the hills, but his horse threw him at Hob's Dell (see later). His pursuers found the horse, took the taxes in its saddlebags for their pains, and slapped the beast back into Norham. Finding no sign of Harald or the sword, they rode straight here and reported to Beorn.

Beorn is all but certain that the sword is lost within the boundary of the Dell and neither it nor the message will ever be found. He would like to make *absolutely* certain, but he is not prepared to risk his own skin and his men will certainly not undertake such a mission. Hence he is employing the player-characters to get the sword back. If they fail to return, he will seek out other adventurers and offer them the same deal. He is very keen to make sure that the loss of the sword does not become widely known. If his fellow plotters got to hear of it, they might decide he was a careless liability and finish him off along with the baron!

II. Getting there

GM: If they leave at once, the characters should reach Norham by noon the following day. They will probably choose to stop overnight at Igham. Farmer Gormand there is an obliging fellow who will let them sleep on his floor for three pennies apiece.

You are advised not to bother with random encounters on the road. This adventure is tough enough!

A day and a half's journey east brings you to Norham. The road is a treacherous muddy track at this time of year (late autumn), and as you pass the village pond you begin to savour thoughts of a hot bath. Perhaps one of the good people of Norham will take you in. They are stout-hearted folk, proud of their freedom and the living they eke out in this tiny farming community. You have heard that they always help wayfarers out of the kindness of their hearts, and never accept payment.

You must have heard wrong. Three men strolling in from the fields glower at you coldly before disappearing into a wide building of stone and timber.

You make your way inside. The air is smoky from the fire in the middle of the building. A cow has been slaughtered and is slowly roasting over the hearth. There are several people here, and among them you quickly pick out the men you saw outside.

"We cannot welcome vagabonds," declares one, stepping up to you. "These are lean times and we are honest working folk. Toil is the most respected virtue in Norham; idle mendicants are given short shrift."

Everyone in the room has fallen silent. They watch you with sullen expressions.

GM: The man they are talking to is Hyple, the head man of the village. If they are to get welcome here, he is the one they must convince of their honest intentions. An offer of money – some ten silver pieces would suffice – will certainly help. Conversely, if the characters resort to threats they may be able to cow the villagers for a time, but they will never get any co-operation. Such co-operation is vital to the adventure.

If they can befriend Hyple, he takes them over by the fire and tries to answer their questions. If he cannot remember some detail personally, he will yell out the question and someone in the room will pipe up with the answer.

> *"The tax collector rode through Norham just before dawn a few days' ago, as though Old Nick himself were right behind. Only a short time later, two men on frothing chargers came pounding through. They must soon have caught up with the first man. Some time later, the tax collector's horse came limping back into the village."*

> Will the smith ambles over with a mug of ale in his hand and takes up the story: *"I caught the poor beast's reins myself. It was stumbling about and rolling its eyes – shivering like it'd been ridden hard all night. Its saddlebags had been slit with a knife, cleaned out but for a few copper pieces."*

> *"The other two men rode back just after that,"* says Hyple. *"They paid none of us any heed, just bantered with one another in the nervous manner of men who've done an evil deed. They glanced at the horse as they rode by, and one of them grinned at the other and patted his saddlebag, but they didn't stop."*

GM: If questioned as to what they suppose happened to Harald, Hyple and the others are of one mind:

> *"There can be no doubt he strayed near Hob's Dell. Either the two men overtook him and butchered him there, or he hid from them in the Dell and Gardener Jack got him. He'll not be seen in this world again."*

117

GM: The characters will surely have a dozen questions on their lips. What and where is the Dell? Who is 'Gardener Jack'? You should paraphrase the villagers' answers from the following folklore:

Hob's Dell is a hollow up in low hills north of Norham Wood. It is enclosed by a fence of sharp iron palings that Saint Ambrosius is said to have put up one Twelfth Night long ago, to keep the evil of the hollow forever trapped inside. The place is permanently shrouded in fog, so that beyond the black railings of the fence one can usually see only a blanket of whiteness. Even on the hottest days of summer the fog maintains its grip on the place – it rolls back from the fence, but is never gone entirely. On such days, the tangled 'garden' within the hollow lies revealed: a clammy, weed-choked place where wisps of sickly white mist move through the long grass like snakes.

'Gardener Jack' is the local name for the monster that lives within the Dell. The villagers speak of him with such conviction that it may be some time before the characters realize that he has not in fact ever been seen by anyone here. There are plenty of stories about how someone's grandfather once caught a glimpse of him at dusk, etc, but no first-hand testimony. Everyone in the village has their own vivid idea of what Jack is – some say he's a wizened dwarf with a giant's head, others that he's a ragged wolf-mawed serpent, or a hairy ogre with a necklace of skulls. (Who can say where such legends come from? The truth, we shall shortly see, is rather different.)

Lastly, like most folklore, the stories about Gardener Jack are rife with inconsistency. He is said to wander the hills in the guise of a man in white robes, and lure travellers into the mists of the Dell. But the iron fence is believed to keep him trapped *within* the Dell, so there is a conundrum here. Furthermore, though the villagers refer to Jack as 'evil' and 'a fiend', they clearly have a sort of affection for him. Though they fear him, he has never brought any of them harm; and he is, after all, their own *local* bugbear!

III. The adventure at Hob's Dell

You remain in Norham overnight and set out for Hob's Dell early the next morning. One of the village boys takes you into the hills and points you on your way before scurrying back towards Norham. Following the signs he described to you, you pass a lightning-split oak and wend your way beside a gurgling brook, and in about an hour you reach Hob's Dell.

A sea of freezing fog hangs here, filling the air with a damp animal reek. You find a fence of iron railings higher than your heads, sturdy despite its rust. Following this a little way, you see a few gaps where the railings are broken or rusted away, though none large enough for a man to squeeze through.

Soon you arrive at the gate in this fence. Close by you notice a possible clue to the tax collector's fate: a bloodied tatter of cloth hangs from one of the fence's sharp spikes.

The gate is fastened shut with a heavy chain on which hangs a large black crucifix. Beyond the railings you see only the impenetrable blanket of the mist. . .

The chain on the gate is in fact the single all-important link in the boundary spell that shackles the evil of the Dell. Under a Mystic's *See Enchantment* power it will thus register as strongly magical. Actually, the fence is not entirely whole; there are some points where it has rusted through, despite the magic invoked when it was erected. But as long as the chain is not removed, Tuannon (the Wight whose abode this is – see later) is unable to escape from the Dell.

The crucifix is tarnished silver. It is quite large – more than forty centimetres – and could conceivably be wielded in combat, like a club. After a single battle it would be left battered and unusable, of course, so the

119

HOB'S DELL

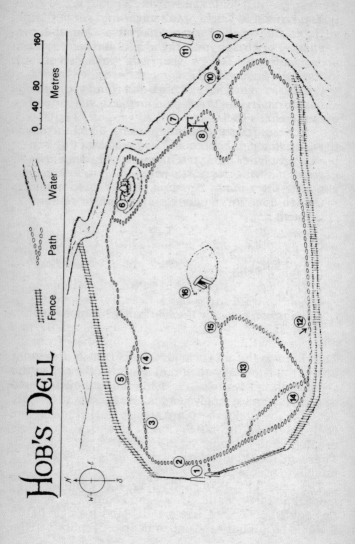

Fence   Path   Water

Metres

0 40 80 160

characters may dismiss the idea of using it as a weapon. Because it is solid silver, it could prove effective against the Wight. Melted down, it would yield silver to the value of some 200 Florins. (All this presupposes, of course, that the characters check it out and discover that it *is* silver. In its tarnished state it looks more like lead.)

Getting into the Dell will not be a problem, even if the characters decide against unfastening the gate. The climb over the fence has a *difficulty factor* of 6. (Only 5, if another character can provide a leg up.) This means that any character with a *Reflexes* score of 6 or higher has no problem scaling it. Others must roll under their *Reflexes* on 1d20; a failed roll means the character slips (20% chance of impaling himself on the railings – treat this like a dagger blow) and must try again.

General notes about the Dell:

(a) The entire region within the Dell is shrouded in thick fog. The characters' visibility will be no more than 30m – and beyond 10m, objects appear only as shadows on the mist. The Wight's vision is not impeded by this fog.

(b) Characters can move at normal speed on the path. That is, 10m per Combat Round normally, and up to 40m/CR when running. If they stray from the path onto the uneven, muddy terrain of the inner Dell, movement rates are halved. Any character running on the rough has a 20% chance each Round of catching his foot in a hole and falling.

(c) The characters will not get lost if they stick to the path. If they lose sight of the path, there is then a 20% chance each minute (ten Combat Rounds) of getting lost. You should not tell them that they are lost – just let them say where they think they're heading, then secretly roll d8 to determine the actual direction. (1 = north, 2 = north-east, 3 = east, etc.)

(d) Locations of particular interest are numbered. This numbering will not necessarily be the order in which the characters come to each location, of course.

1. A monk at peace?

Among the tangled weeds bordering the Dell you see a cracked stone slab. The resemblance to a sarcophagus is unmistakable. Some words are carved into the face of the slab, so badly weathered that you can hardly make them out:
QUIESCO MANEO CUSTODIO
  Do you want to open it. . .?

The task of lifting the lid has a *difficulty factor* of 35. This means that several characters whose combined *Strength* totals at least 35 can lift it. Each must deduct 1 *Health Point* for the exertion.

If they open it, they can see immediately that it is indeed a sarcophagus. Little remains of the occupant now: just a clutch of mouldered bones. They have no way of knowing that these are the mortal remains of the saintly Ambrosius (see later). He fell ill as work on the fence was nearing completion. His last instruction to his followers was to inter him here, so that his spirit might keep watch and see that Tuannon Dûr never escaped from his imprisonment.

If any of the players express the opinion that this is the grave of a good or holy person, take them aside for a moment. Tell them that they feel in their hearts that they are truly gazing upon the bones of a saint. (Whether or not they wish to pass on this revelation to the others is up to them.) If any of the player-characters who receive this revelation are Knights, remind them that it is the custom for Knights in this medieval world to keep saintly relics. The tooth or finger-bone of a saint, stored within the pommel of the Knight's sword, is highly prized for the luck it brings its owner. Any

122

character who takes a relic of Ambrosius now and stores it in the pommel of his sword will get a + 1 bonus to both DEFENCE and MAGICAL DEFENCE whenever he is under attack from undead beings.

2. A trail of blood

A rust coloured smear lies across the stones of the path. It is level with the blood-soaked scrap of cloth you noticed on the fence. It seems that the tax collector – if it was he – was badly wounded and crawled across the path into the interior of the Dell.

The player-characters will never learn exactly what happened to Harald, but the true facts are these. Harald saw that Beorn's men were gaining on him. A Knight of considerable prowess, he felt that he might stand his ground and defeat them both. Ordinarily he would have done so, but not with his lord's life in the balance. At all costs he had to reach the castle, so he turned off the road just beyond Norham and tried to shake off his pursuers in the wooded hills.

He found a misty nook by the mysterious iron fence of Hob's Dell. Behind and below, his pursuers' angry curses drifted through the pre-dawn. He had lost them.

Suddenly a figure stepped out of the fog right in front of him: a druid with a look of wild madness in his eyes. Harald's horse, sensing evil magic, reared back in terror. Harald himself was thrown back over the fence into Hob's Dell, gashing his arm to the bone on a sharp paling and landing heavily on his back. The two men had heard the horse's terrified whinney and were drawing near. With a broken collarbone and terrible wound, Harald could not hope to stand against them; he could not even climb the fence out of the Dell. Enraged at his helplessness, he crawled painfully away from the fence, into the thick enshrouding fog. . .

3. The restless dead

> *You are walking on a firm path of sharp flints, but the ground to either side is a coarse heath of puddles and snaggled roots. Suddenly a patch of earth beside the path shudders. The turf splits and soil is pushed back as a ghastly livid-hued figure rises from its shallow grave. It watches you for a moment with empty, unblinking eyes. Then it hefts its spear and lurches towards you. . .*

This was a traveller who wandered too near to Hob's Dell. It is now one of several Zombies that Tuannon has planted at points around his 'garden'.

First ZOMBIE

ATTACK 10   Spear (2d4 + 1, 5 points)
DEFENCE 4   Armour Factor 0
MAGICAL DEFENCE 1   Movement: 5m/CR
EVASION 1   Reflexes 3
Health Points 15

The characters could easily escape from the Zombie. If they do, you will have to keep track of its position; it will shuffle along after them and return to its grave after completing one circuit of the Dell. All the other Zombies in the scenario behave like this, so if the player-characters make a habit of running away they could end up with quite a band of the monsters out looking for them.

Remember to note down any Zombies that the characters 'kill'. If they later enter the barrow, the Wight will summon any surviving Zombies to protect him.

4. A burnished blade

(This is visible only from the southern branch of the path:)

A naked sword lies in the moist grass just off the path. Its blade points away from you, untarnished; its hilt is wound with gold wire. The undergrowth where it lies seems somehow wholesome — the weeds and sickly fungi of the rest of the Dell shun this sword.

It is a +1 enchanted sword.

It is incidentally pointing in the direction of the sundial (see 13).

5. Another zombie

In a shower of pebbles and earth, a grisly Zombie pushes its way up from the ground just behind you. Your footsteps have roused it from its dreamless sleep. It swings its mold-clumped axe at the rear-most character in the party.

Since this Zombie is attacking from behind, give it 3 chances in 6 of achieving surprise on the characters.

Second ZOMBIE

ATTACK 10   Axe (d8 + 1, 7 points)
DEFENCE 4   Armour Factor 1
MAGICAL DEFENCE 1   Movement: 5m/CR
EVASION 1   Reflexes 6
Health Points 17

6. An eerie isle

A foul stench reaches your nostrils. A few metres further on, you discover its source — the mists part to reveal a slime-covered stagnant pond. In the middle of the pond you can see a small island where trees grow in twisted forms and trail their roots in the mucky water.

Suddenly a flight of huge bats pour from the gnarled branches and soar towards you like phantoms through the mist.

These are ordinary Bats. Any character bitten by one has a chance (01–05 on d100) of contracting a degenerative illness that will cause him to lose 1–4 *Reflexes* points permanently, unless he receives a *Cure Disease* spell within one month.

BATS
ATTACK 11   Bite (d3, 1 point)
DEFENCE 9   Armour Factor 0
MAGICAL DEFENCE 2
EVASION 6
Health Points:

First Bat	1 HP	Seventh Bat	1 HP
Second Bat	1 HP	Eighth Bat	1 HP
Third Bat	1 HP	Ninth Bat	1 HP
Fourth Bat	1 HP	Tenth Bat	1 HP
Fifth Bat	1 HP	Eleventh Bat	1 HP
Sixth Bat	1 HP	Twelfth Bat	1 HP

7. The river

A river flows down from the north. Presumably it leads into Norham Wood and eventually joins the Hern River some miles to the east. A few thin tendrils of mist drift above the rushing water; the far bank seems clear.

This river forms part of Ambrosius' boundary spell, which is why the fog comes to such an abrupt end here.

8. A grisly find

A high pole looms out of the mist. From its crossbar hangs a stark corpse, swinging in chains and

shackles. He wears the livery of the baron, torn at the shoulder to reveal a gaping blood-caked wound. There is no other mark of injury on him.

One arm is twisted up behind him, its white fingers still clamped around a fine sword he had slung on his back. It seems he died before he had time to draw it. You find it strange that he did not reach for the other sword he wears – scabbarded at his belt, it would have been more accessible.

This is, of course, Harald the tax collector. He encountered the Wight (see later) and could do nothing to defend himself from its enervating grip. After draining Harald of his strength, the Wight hung him on the gibbet to die, intending later to transform him into a Zombie. Alone, wracked with pain and knowing that his last hours were upon him, Harald mustered all his will and forced his numb fingers to close on the swordhilt. Thus, even in death, he may reveal Beorn's treachery.

The hilt of the sword can be unscrewed. Within is a small parchment that reads: 'Alcuin – The old wolf's days are numbered! Grisaille and Montombre are with us. I shall be visiting Ulric. Ensure the castle is guarded by our own men on the day of the hunt. Your brother, Beorn.' This concerns the murder of the baron, planned for two weeks hence. If it came to light, this document would be enough to put Beorn's head on the chopping-block, along with his co-conspirators.

Harald's money-pouch contains 20 silver Florins.

9. An Elfin maid

You are hailed from the far bank of the river. A slender girl all in green stands there, a bow on her back and an elegant sword at her thigh. Her fine features and pointed ears mark her clearly as an Elf.

129

"Do you know that you wander in Tuannon's garden?" she calls out. *"I would not recommend it. He is apt to sow your bodies in the cold ground."*

The Elf is Taliriana, a 2nd rank Sorceress. She knows a little of the history of the Dell (see later), and may relate some of this to the player-characters.

Taliriana, while not truly malicious, has a heartless sense of humour. She will try to entice the characters to walk north along the bank and cross the river via the stepping stones (see 10). . .

10. Stones across the water

Seven large flat stepping stones lead across the river. Beyond, high up on the far bank, stands a stone cross atop a tall column.

Roll d100. On a roll of 01 – 10 the characters will notice something strange about the stones – they do not throw up spray from the flowing river, the swirls of mist do not eddy around them, etc. This is because they are *Images* cast by Taliriana (see 9).

If anyone tries to cross, the stepping stone will vanish as soon as he lands on it and he will plunge into the river. He must roll under his *Reflexes* score on d20 to scramble back to the bank. A character who is not wearing any armour gets four attempts at this before the current buffets him under; a character in leather armour gets two attempts; a character wearing ring mail, chainmail or plate gets one roll and then, if he is not out, gets swept under. Once submerged, the character may still struggle desperately to get to the bank. If unarmoured, he must roll under his *Reflexes* on 1d20; if in leather, he must make the roll on 3d20; if in heavier armour, the required roll is made on 6d20! Once submerged, the character can survive for a number of Combat Rounds equal to his *Strength*. He may wish to get out of his armour; this takes ten

130

Combat Rounds – and means, of course, that the character loses his armour at the bottom of the river.

While all this is going on, Taliriana's musical laughter will ring out as she disappears among the trees across the river.

11. Stone cross

This monument reinforces the boundary spell along the entire river bank. Even if the fence warding is breached (by the removal of the silver chain), the Wight will not be able to ford the river.

12. A rusting glaive

An iron shod halberd lies on the ground some distance from the path. Tendrils of dead ivy are wound about it, and it is pock-marked with rust.

A curse has been laid on this abominable weapon. Any character who lifts it from the ground is assailed by the curse with a MAGICAL ATTACK of 20. The effect of the curse is to cause the character to dissolve into the pall of fog covering Hob's Dell. This curse is repeated every round until the character drops the halberd.

The blade of the halberd is pointing directly away from the sundial at 13.

13. A sundial

You approach a curious stone plinth. Pulling away the net of ivy that covers it, you discover that it is an ancient sundial. Under a green film of lichen, the carved numerals glint with inlaid gold. The gnomon is of bronze; the end of it was possibly sculpted to represent an animal's head, but it is so badly corroded that you cannot tell what animal this was.

If the lichen is scraped off the dial, a faint inscription is revealed: DECUS ET TUTAMEN

The gnomon can be removed from the dial. A small cavity lies beneath, in which rests a jewel: a sparkling yellow gem encircled by a band of gold. Cryptic words are engraven upon this: 'Sunlight, banish. Sky-jewel, sear.'

Make sure you know who is holding this jewel at all times. If the character with the jewel recites the inscription on it, one of two things happens:

Daytime – The mist rolls back to a distance of 20m from the jewel. Sunlight streams down. If the Wight is nearby when this happens, he will flee back to his barrow in terror.

Nighttime (or within the barrow) – The jewel bursts into a brilliant flare of light. Any undead within 20m will be stunned (unable to attack or defend) for 1 – 6 Combat Rounds.

The magic of the jewel works only once, and then it crumbles into fine ash. It was left by Ambrosius, and its powers do not function outside the Dell.

The carved numerals of the dial are indeed inlaid with gold, but not deeply. By chiselling assiduously with a knife, a character might get ten Florins' worth.

14. Yet another zombie

You are approaching a point where four paths come together. A pebble rolls across the path ahead of you. A twitching hand, covered with bloodless sores, emerges from the ground. Before you can react, a snaggle-toothed Zombie has risen up to attack you.

This Zombie is another of those (see 3 and 5) that the Wight of Hob's Dell uses as his sentries.

Third ZOMBIE

ATTACK 10   Morning Star (d6 + 1, 6 points)
DEFENCE 4   Armour Factor 0
MAGICAL DEFENCE 1   Movement: 5m/CR
EVASION 1   Reflexes 2
Health Points 17

15. The last zombie

Two paths join into one leading east. Evil is strong in the very air here. You shudder at a horrible moan that seems to come from out of the ground nearby. You turn to behold a hulking Zombie clawing out of its grave. It wears a few scraps of rusting armour and wields a massive halberd.

Tuannon has kept the most powerful of the Zombies to guard the approach to his barrow.

Fourth ZOMBIE

ATTACK 10   Halberd (d10 + 1, 6 points)
DEFENCE 4   Armour Factor 2
MAGICAL DEFENCE 1   Movement: 5m/CR
EVASION 1   Reflexes 2
Health Points 24

16. The Wight's barrow

A large tumulus, surely one of the burial mounds of ages past, lies ahead of you. In its steep, grass-clad sides, roughly hewn slabs of rock frame the entrance tunnel. It seems like a gaping black mouth, seeping noxious vapours into the air of the Dell.

Five blue-stained skulls have been placed nearby — one atop the entrance and two to either side. As you draw near, their jaws open and they begin to chatter and shriek!

The skulls are those of Tuannon's five thanes who elected to remain here with their king's body (see below). Their terrible clamouring alerts him that intruders are close at hand, and he will begin to make his way here from the burial chamber. (*Exception*: if the characters broke Ambrosius' boundary spell, Tuannon would have sensed this at once. In this case he will be already waiting for them.) The characters will be able to hear the skulls' shrieking even within the barrow, and it will cease only when Tuannon is dead — or when they are.

Who is, or was, Tuannon? The player-characters may never learn the story, unless Taliriana told them part of it. You might like to have some of the rest related to them by a Non-Player Character in a subsequent adventure.

Interlude: The history of Hob's Dell

They call him 'Gardener Jack' now, a bugbear that the women of Norham use to frighten their disobedient children. But he was a king in this land a thousand years ago — the grim Tuannon Dûr, warlord of five thousand men. When the legions came, Tuannon put on woad and led his army in one bloody battle after another. He piled the skulls of slain legionnaries high at the foot of his throne. Finally the crack VIth legion came against him, with the legendary Flavius Venturo at its head. His army was outmanoeuvred and broken, but Tuannon himself escaped with his druids and a handful of veterans, and carried on the unrelenting 'guerilla war' against the invaders for many years.

When Tuannon finally died, his druids and loyal warriors carried him up to a secluded hollow in the wooded hills and laid his body to rest in a secret barrow. Five of the men, grown old with their king, chose to remain there with him.

Tuannon had died, but some part of him would not lie buried while outsiders dwelt in the land of his birth. Perhaps mystical forces worked upon him, perhaps it was only his implacable warrior ways that could not allow him to rest – by whatever reason, he arose from his barrow as a Wight and haunted the region thereabouts for many years. Even after the legions had departed, recalled to defend their crumbling empire, there were other invaders from other lands. Travellers learned to shun the vicinity of Norham Wood, and many fireside tales were whispered of the bleak-visaged Wight that roamed the misty hills.

Four hundred years ago, a holy man was lodging at the village now called Hesard's Ford and heard these tales. Ambrosius determined to put an end to the evil. Calling his followers together, he took them up into the hills. The fog, it is said, drew back from the hills and the Wight hid in his barrow like an old wolf in its den. Wise Ambrosius knew he could never drive out Tuannon's presence entirely, for the Wight was one with the mists and stones of the land. Instead, he pent in the evil with an iron fence, and set a holy seal upon the gate.

Since that day, the Wight has chafed at his imprisonment. He yearns for vengeance on all living things. He cannot leave the Dell, but he can cast his spells a little way beyond it. (It was his *Mirage* that scared Harald's steed.) Norham Wood has remained a place of ill repute.

17. Entrance tunnel

The interior of the barrow is unlit and thick with mist. Even when their lanterns and/or torches are lit, the characters will be able to see no further than 5m.

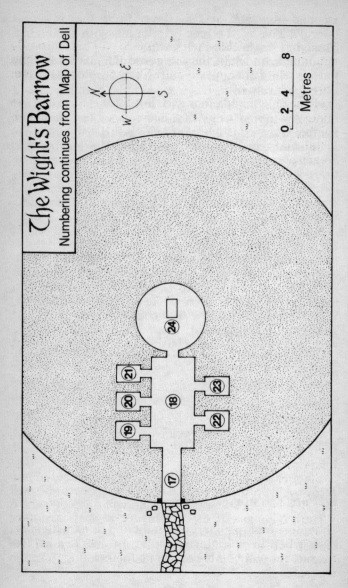

The Wight's Barrow

Numbering continues from Map of Dell

0 2 4 8

Metres

18. The Long Chamber

Though it is possible the characters will have already run into Tuannon (if they removed the chain from the gate — see 16), they are most likely to encounter him here.

He seems to glide forward, a tall figure against the mist. A large silver clasp bearing a horned, pagan symbol fastens his heavy red cloak at the shoulder. He is thin and grey, with eyes like ice. On his dead brow he wears a crown of holly.

TUANNON DÛR, the Wight of Hob's Dell

ATTACK 17   Two-handed Sword (d10, 5
DEFENCE 10   points)
            Javelin (d6, 4 points)

MAGICAL ATTACK 20
MAGICAL DEFENCE 10   Armour Factor 0
                      (but with partial
                      immunity to non-
                      magical weapons)

EVASION 3
Health Points 20

The Wight has the powers of a 5th rank Mystic, and also four special spells that he is able to use once each day: *Apparitions, Mephitic Breath, Portal* and *Raise Fog*. See DRAGON WARRIORS Book One for full details of these spells.

His weaponry consists of his sword and two javelins.

If the characters flee from him, he will pursue them to the edge of the Dell — and beyond, if they broke the boundary spell.

Slaying Tuannon in this form will not get rid of him forever. Eventually, within weeks or months, he will return as a Ghost. Years later he will have become a Wraith. This has no direct bearing on the characters — they will be long gone by then — but is the reason why it is best never to break the boundary spell. As long as there are invaders in his homeland, Tuannon will remain. . .

19. – 23. Side chambers

A headless skeleton lies on a large shield in each of these rooms. These are the five thanes whose skulls stand watch outside the barrow.

They will *not* rise up to attack the characters. These are skeletons of the properly dead and inactive variety.

24. Main burial chamber

Behind the long stone slab on which his body was laid to rest are strewn Tuannon's mortuary treasures:

Item	Worth
an electrum torc	250 Florins
two silver wristbands	35 Florins each
a gold ring	30 Florins
an emerald set in a copper diadem	170 Florins

Besides this, there was the silver clasp on his cloak. That has a value of some 30 Florins.

IV. Wrapping up

Weary after your adventure, you begin to trudge down towards Norham. After a short distance you hear voices ahead. Peering around a tree, you see Beorn and two other men waiting in the lane.

The characters must think fast. The easiest and safest course is to hand Beorn the sword he wants (if they have it). He will destroy the document, pay them the remainder of their fee, and that will be the end of the matter.

If they try to turn the tables on Beorn, they must be more careful. Any attempt to hide the document and then blackmail him will probably result in a lingering death. Beorn's reasoning is that if they are dead they cannot testify against him, and any testimony is worthless if they cannot produce the document.

In the event of a fight here in the lane, the two henchmen will fight on foot. Beorn, having a warhorse, will fight from the saddle – at the same time characters are meleeing him, his horse will be able to kick and bite them.

First HENCHMAN: (1st rank Knight)	ATTACK 13 DEFENCE 7	MAGICAL DEFENCE 3 EVASION 4	*Health Points* 11
Second HENCHMAN (1st rank Knight)	ATTACK 13 DEFENCE 7	MAGICAL DEFENCE 3 EVASION 4	*Health Points* 10
BEORN (3rd rank Knight)	ATTACK 15 DEFENCE 9	MAGICAL DEFENCE 5 EVASION 4	*Health Points* 14

All are armed with sword and shield and wear chainmail armour.

Beorn's WARHORSE	ATTACK 17 DEFENCE 4 Kick (d8, 6 points)	MAGICAL DEFENCE 3 EVASION 4	*Health Points* 20 Armour Factor 0

If the characters evade them, Beorn and his men will ride on to Karickbridge and lie in wait there. The characters, anticipating such a strategy, could leave the road and travel cross-country. They would then have to pass either through the marshes around Fenring Forest or the menacing Jewelspider Wood. By the time they reach the castle, Beorn and his henchmen will have returned. The characters will need some ingenious plan to reach the baron and place the incriminating document into his hands.

To summarize: the characters may hand the document to Beorn, in which case they get their remaining 100 Florins and have to relinquish 90% of any treasure they brought out of the Dell. Or they can somehow get the document to the baron. This entails great perils, but they should be richly rewarded – at least 100 Florins each, and the opportunity to become his retainers if they wish.

Suggested experience awards: 5 experience points per character for completing the adventure in Hob's Dell, plus any appropriate experience for defeating opponents. If they discover the document in the sword and successfully get it to the baron, each character should get an additional 3 experience points.

HUNTER'S MOON

(Co-written by Robert Dale)

General note: An adventure which can be run as a follow-up to *A Shadow On the Mist*.

Overview of the adventure: The characters are travelling north with the baron when his ship is forced to shelter in a cove to effect repairs. A ruined citadel stands nearby, and the characters are sent to ensure no dangers reside there which might threaten the baron and his retinue.

I. Background

GM: This adventure is designed to follow *A Shadow On The Mist* as part of an ongoing campaign. It can be made to dovetail with the earlier adventure in one of two ways:

(i) If the player-characters uncovered Beorn's treachery and revealed it to the baron, they will be rewarded. The baron has invited them to join his retinue on the trip to Port Beltayn, and is considering bestowing the honour of being his permanent retainers if they perform well on this mission.

(ii) If Beorn's plot was not revealed, he will still be alive. In this case, it is he who has brought the player-characters along on the journey. Somehow he hopes to sabotage the mission — perhaps even slay the baron, if the opportunity presents itself. He will either try to bring the player-characters into the conspiracy or else engineer events so that they take the blame for anything that goes awry.

II. The beginning

None but the bravest or most desperate of men would risk a passage north to Port Beltayn in midwinter. Storms make the rocky islands of the White Coast still more dangerous than usual, and there is no truly secure anchorage between Clyster – where you embarked – and Beltayn. Yet you find yourselves in the retinue of Baron Aldred, riding out a snarling gale off Cape Calegon at a time when you would much prefer to be feasting in his Great Hall and celebrating the turn of the year.

This is a mission of crucial importance to the baron. Duke Carnasse, with whom he hopes to strike an alliance against his foes to the south, is spending the winter in Beltayn. Thus, though the journey is perilous, it must be made.

Eventually the storm abates, but the Linden has lost her mast and is taking on water. The crew man the oars and take her in to shore. Baron Aldred consults with the captain. They look towards a line of fir trees along the coast, obviously intending to beach nearby and gather timber to rig a jurymast for the last leg to Port Beltayn.

As the Linden finds a sheltered bay, you are startled to sight a ruined citadel, half flooded by the tide, along the coast. As the ship makes shore, the baron calls you to him.

"There may be brigands or goblins in yonder citadel," he says. "We would not wish to be ambushed while making our repairs. Investigate the citadel. Slay whatever dangerous creatures lurk there, but return and report to me if you encounter men or overwhelming force. Salvage anything of value."

Thus, hearts high with the thought of gold and adventure and the hope of your lord's bounty, you set out. . .

III. The citadel

*An hour's brisk march through the dense snow-
clad woodland brings you to the walls of the
ancient citadel. Built of monolithic blocks of lime-
stone, the place is of a strange architecture you
find utterly alien.*

*Stepping between the broken timbers of the
gate, your awe and fear grow ever stronger. This
is truly a place of death. Strewn about the
entrance and across the plaza are countless
mouldered bones, rusting weapons and armour.*

*In the shadow of the arch sits an old man clad in
rags. His thin hair waves in the icy breeze, his
blind eyes stare out beyond you, across the forest-
ed land.*

GM: As the characters approach, the old man will
inform them that he keeps the gate of this citadel of
Karvala until the return of its lord. If questioned
further, he will tell the following tale:

"Centuries ago, Lord Karvala and his ninety sons
were driven by evil sorcery from their homeland, and a
geas placed upon them that they wander the waste
until they could raise a hall not on the earth nor in the
sea, not in fire nor in air. After years of journeying,
Lord Karvala saw a child building a castle of sand on
this strand and, thanking the great gods for their sign,
built his hall on land that was neither of the earth nor
of the sea. At the last he surrounded the hall with a
high wall to keep back the sea. Here he dwelt with his
sons, and the sons of his sons.

"From across the sea there came a new people, with
new laws and new gods. Karvala took himself to his
tower and shut himself within, saying that he must pon-
der how to punish these sea-pests. But the invaders
bewitched him so that he fell into a deep sleep and
could not aid his people. And they set wards about his
tower, and locks of magic upon its doors, and slew his

142

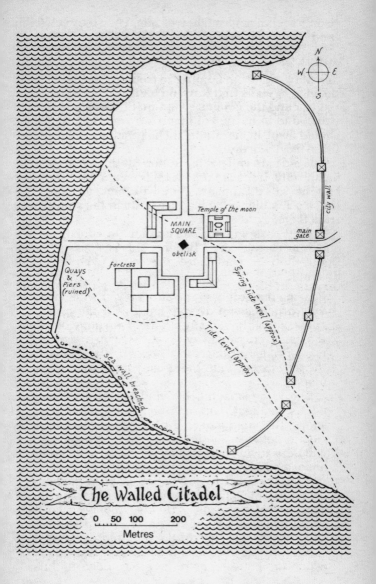

The Walled Citadel

0   50   100   200

Metres

people so that none might free him. Then they ruled this land many scores of years.

"But the gods were enraged that the one they had chosen to rule should be thus set aside. They sent fire and plague and earthquake to trouble the citadel, until the mighty walls that Karvala had built fell at last, and the sea and the goblins swept in. Still Karvala did not wake, and in honour of him it was decreed that none should dwell in his citadel till he comes again to choose those most worthy."

The old man will not try to stop the characters entering the city. If they reach for their weapons or threaten him, he will disappear. They will then see, some distance off, a black dog leaping through the ruins away from them.

If they pass without causing him to vanish, he has one thing more to say: "Begone. This is a cursed place. Death lies in wait here for those who love not Karvala."

Passing the gate into the citadel, you walk into a long processional avenue lined with the broken ruins of mighty buildings. Rubble partially blocks the wide carriageway, and there are signs of widespread burning. More bones are scattered in the wreckage, but these may or may not be human.

The citadel is full of shadows in the weak winter sunlight, and high clouds threaten more snow. The wind makes a constant keening as it rushes between the fallen columns. A large seagull flaps away, alarmed by your approach. Your unease builds as you near the main square.

A black obelisk twelve paces broad at the base dominates the square. Its surface is covered with geometrical patterns, entwined glyphs, and a script whose like you have never seen. The air is tense with the watchful calm that presages danger. If this obelisk is the tower of Karvala to which the gatekeeper referred, you can find no

144

sign of any doorway.

About the square stand more buildings ravaged by fire and decay, all of the same monolithic construction. Two structures strike you as especially interesting. The first is a small hexagonal edifice with a domed roof, set atop a large square plinth. The other is a fortress with four massive square towers.

Your eyes catch a movement. Someone was standing at a high window of the fortress, and ducked back as you looked up!

IV. The fortress

The wreckage of wide wooden gates block the entrance to the fortress. Clambering through the broken timber, you come into a courtyard surrounded by scorched walls and choked with battered masonry upon which may be seen long fronds of dried seaweed. A few stagnant pools add to the air of desolation.

The block surrounding the courtyard is reduced to a gutted shell, but the four towers are marginally more intact. You approach the entrance to the nothernmost tower, where you saw signs of life. Or thought you did.

The entrance tunnel is low, and the stairwell of the tower damp – and dark, despite gaping holes in the walls and roof. A decayed staircase sweeps up to the first floor balcony. A woman in a white gown stands there watching you.

GM: The woman is in fact a Spectre, though the translucence of her form is not apparent in the semi-darkness. She says nothing, and if the characters call up to her she merely turns and moves away.

Her intention is to lure them onto the stairs, which are unsafe and will collapse under their weight. When this happens, the characters on the stairs will plummet 1 – 6 metres. The Spectre will then scream horribly and leap to attack. It is at this point that you should roll for its *fright attack* and chance of surprising them as they struggle free of the rubble.

SPECTRE

> ATTACK 19   Touch (d12, 5 points)
> DEFENCE 12   Armour Factor 0 (but unaffected by nonmagic weapons)
> MAGICAL DEFENCE 11   Movement: 12m/CR
> EVASION 4   *Reflexes*: 15
> *Health Points* 8

Any character who climbs up to the balcony is taking a risk – there is a 40% chance that it, like the stairs, will give way and cause him to drop 6m into the stair-well below. Hidden in an alcove off the balcony is the Spectre's treasure: a silver-chased black wood drum and a pewter cup with gems set all around the rim.

These are both magical items. If the drum is taken to a place on the coast and someone starts to pound it, it will summon an eldritch longboat manned by silent oarsmen with long seaweed-matted beards and skins blue with cold. The longboat arrives within fifteen minutes of beginning the drumbeat, and will then convey the drummer and up to six companions to anywhere they wish to go. The oarsmen row tirelessly and (as the superstitious will surely guess) are not truly alive.

Eight gems are set around the rim of the cup. Seven are a dull red, but the last glows brightly. If the cup is turned, the glow moves on to another of the gems. With experimentation, the characters will discover that it is always the gem facing to the north that glows. This cup could thus function as a crude compass, and could be sold as such for up to 4000 Florins.

The rest of the fortress is structurally unsafe, and the characters will soon realize there is nothing to be gained from lingering here.

The Temple of the Moon

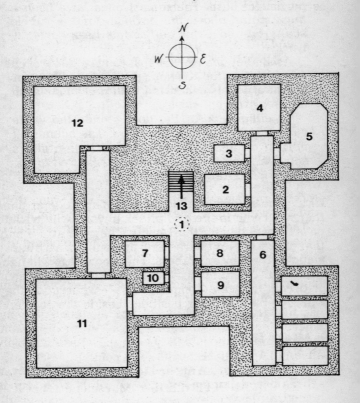

| Stairs (arrow points down) | Door | Bottom of newel stairway | Metres |

V. The Temple of the Moon

Across the main square, north-east of the black obelisk, stands a hexagonal pavilion atop a flat pyramidal base. There must once have been a huge statue above the pavilion, for the rubble scattered about this edifice has been carefully worked.

Ascending the worn steps, you see the broken feet of this statue still flank the pavilion. The door ahead of you is decorated with a grinning skull above a crescent moon.

To either side of the door stands the white marble statue of a large hound. The hounds sit upright on their haunches higher than a man's shoulder, and their stone gums are bared to display wicked fangs.

GM: The statues are Moon Dogs, magical guardians that will come to life and attack anyone who tries to pass them and enter the Temple. They will attack only that character (or characters) and will ignore attacks made on them by any others. The Moon Dogs will fight until slain, or until their victim(s) is dead, unconscious or driven from the Temple steps – whereupon they will lope back to their positions beside the door and revert to stone.

MOON DOGS

> ATTACK 18   Bite (d8 + 1, 5 points)
> DEFENCE 4   Armour Factor 6
> MAGICAL DEFENCE 10   Movement: 12m/CR
> EVASION 4   running: 25/CR
> *Reflexes*: both 14
> *Health Points* both 23 *HP** Rank-equivalent: 6th

(*They automatically heal back up to normal *HP* every time they revert to their stone form.)

148

Assuming that the characters find some way to pass the Moon Dogs and enter the Temple:

You enter a large hexagonal chamber, the roof of which is domed and glass-like. The floor is elaborately incised with spiral patterns enclosing circles of coloured stone. In the centre of the room, a large slab is tilted up revealing a staircase which winds downwards.

Beside the slab are three skeletal corpses. One wears scraps of ceremonial vestments and clutches an ebony-and-silver staff in its fingers.

Noticing score-marks on the floor, you infer that heavy fitments were ransacked from this chamber.

GM: Any character who touches the staff will suffer a Curse with a MAGICAL ATTACK of 25.

The newel staircase leads down to the underworld section of the Temple – the priestly quarters and the cult's inner chambers. Looters have penetrated even here; the characters will discover smashed pottery, splintered wood and a scattering of silver coins as they descend the steps.

1. The foot of the stairs

You descend to the bottom of the newel staircase. Old bones and riven armour lie tangled here. Picking your way across the debris, you find yourselves at the intersection of two 3m wide corridors.

Looking north, you see a wide flight of steps leading down to a heavy mahogany portal. There are no doors along the east and west branches of the corridor that you can see, but when you shine your lantern south it falls upon two doors only a few metres from where you are standing.

GM: If they choose to explore the rooms of the under-world, they might of course do so in any order. Brief notes are given for you to create a description.

2. Living quarters

The door stands ajar. Within you find the rotted remnants of clothing and furniture. A large iron-bound chest stands in one corner of the room.

GM: The chest was booby-trapped, being set to release a poisonous snake as soon as anyone touched the hasp. The mechanism of the trap is long since rusted, the snake long dead. Whatever items were stored inside the chest have been consumed by mould and the centuries. . .

3. Store-room

This room contains the remains of spades, buckets and other tools. In the midst of the debris lies a skeleton with a corroded spear beneath its fingers.

4. Living quarters

GM: This room is similar to 2, but there is no chest.

5. Robes and ritual artifacts

Broken demon-masks and ceremonial staves and adjuncts are strewn across the floor here. There are further signs of looting, and the bones of defenders and despoilers lie intertwined. One skeleton wears fragments of a silvered head-dress, and on its finger is a white gold ring in which is set a chip of jade.

GM: The ring is a *Ring of Agonizing Doom* with six charges. The other artifacts in the room include some silver chalices and bowls worth a total of 500 Florins. They feel evil to the touch, and will not fetch such a price until purified by a cleric.

6. The cells

The corridors you traverse are wide and well-paved even though the floors are cracked in places by an ancient earthquake. Carvings in low relief adorn all the walls, showing life within the citadel in its heyday, full of life and vigour. Wars against barbarian tribes are depicted in detail, and the spoils of victory are seen being carried by many captives.

This corridor ends with four barred cells, within which you see the mouldering remains of many chained captives. They must have starved to death centuries ago – a terrible punishment for who knows what crimes? It is a dismal place, and you swiftly return northwards.

7. Dormitory

This room shows signs of having been the living quarters of several men. The damp rotted wood of eight pallets are arranged along the room.

8. Dormitory

GM: This is similar to the room opposite, except that a tapestry hangs along the southern wall. This has remained curiously untouched by the passage of the years. It is embroidered with ghastly scenes of human sacrifice, necromancy and still more obscene prac-

152

tices. These rites are being conducted beneath a gibbous moon from which a pale-skinned demon has come down. The demon has the body of an androgynous humanoid, but from its neck and wrists grow writhing hooded snakes.

So horrible and heavy with evil is this noxious tapestry that any who attempt to destroy it are subject to a MAGICAL ATTACK of 15 which, if successful, drives the victim insane with terror. The insanity can be cured with *Dispel Magic*, but even then the character will always be beset by qualmy unease whenever he beholds the moon in the sky. . .

9. Library

The decayed shelves of this room once held carved stone plaques. These are now just splintered fragments underfoot. Looking more closely at a large piece of one of the plaques, you see that it was once covered with small carved script that you have no hope nor wish to read.

10. Devotional room

GM: This small chamber is bare of adornment except for a silver crescent-moon motif on the western wall. It was where the priests came for solitary prayer to the less bloodthirsty aspect of their many-natured deity.

11. Secondary cult room

You reach a large mahogany portal at the end of the passage and swing it open. Beyond lies a large vaulted chamber full of ritual paraphernalia – sceptres, masks, bells, drums, rotted vestments. In the crumbling racks that once lined the walls you find a few scroll-cases.

GM: The scrolls are worm-eaten and unreadable. Other items in the room include some vessels of precious metals and gems which could be sold for up to 100 Florins, once purified of their 'evil' taint.

12. Main cult room

You enter a wide pillared chamber. Nine warrior Skeletons stand waiting to greet you, with silvered scimitars in their bony hands and wide deathly grins on their fleshless faces. Each wears a silver torc about its neck and a serpentine wristband of silver coiled about its left arm.

GM: The Skeletons will not attack at once. They point with their scimitars towards the door through which the characters have just entered. If the characters turn around, the Skeletons escort them to the steps down to the charnel-house (see 13). Otherwise, they close and attack.

SKELETONS

ATTACK 11	Scimitars (d8, 4 points)
DEFENCE 5	Armour Factor 0 (but 2 vs stabbing weapons)
MAGICAL DEFENCE 3	Movement: 10m/CR
EVASION 3	*Reflexes: all 12*

Health Points:

First SKELETON	2 *HP*
Second SKELETON	2 *HP*
Third SKELETON	3 *HP*
Fourth SKELETON	3 *HP*
Fifth SKELETON	4 *HP*
Sixth SKELETON	4 *HP*
Seventh SKELETON	5 *HP*
Eighth SKELETON	5 *HP*
Ninth SKELETON	7 *HP*

When each Skeleton is destroyed, the snake-band around its wrist will grow and become a real snake

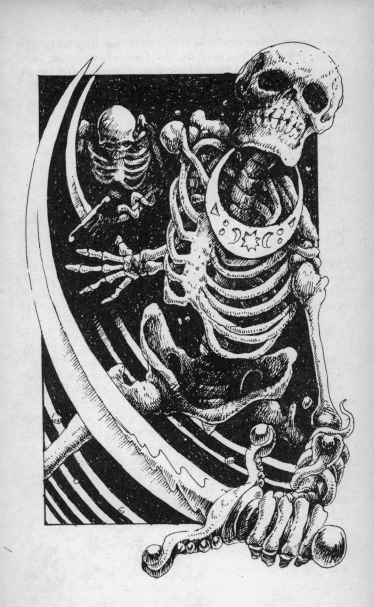

that waits coiled over the fallen remains, hissing at any who approach. These are in fact merely illusions, and can do no harm to the characters. The silver torcs are worth 60 Florins each.

Once they have destroyed all the Skeletons:

> *You look around the room these undead creatures were guarding. On the floor beside a pattern of painted designs and small brass censers lie two long-dead bodies in rotted robes. They hold ritual staves, and appear to have been slain in the middle of some ceremony.*

GM: The priests had summoned a demonic entity just before the reavers burst in and slew them. The demon has remained pent within the confines of the painted designs ever since. If any character enters the pattern he will break the binding spell, releasing the demon. Immediately there will be a rush of wind and darkness, accompanied by an unholy shriek of glee. Everyone within the room at this time suffers a *fright attack* of 2d6 intensity. The demon then returns to its own plane of existence, taking with it the unfortunate souls of any slain by its *fright attack*.

The soulless bodies left behind will arise as Ghouls within three days if not cremated or buried on consecrated ground before then.

The ritual equipment within the room is worth about 200 Florins, though once again it requires purification before this value can be realized.

One of the staves is similar to the one in the hexagonal chamber above, with identical effect if touched. The other is of silver birchwood, and can be used by a Sorcerer to cast *Illusion* and *Phantasm* spells at half the normal *Magic Point* cost.

13. Ossuary

You begin to make your way down a flight of cracked and rubble-choked steps towards a large black door. Niches in the walls contain skeletal remains, and you realise you are passing through the charnel-house of the temple.

Reaching the door, you find it to be twisted within its frame and stained by sea water at the bottom. Water must seep through here at the spring tide.

A heavy bar of black stone secures the door in place. You cannot read the fearsome sigils inlaid in silver along it, but they seem to be warning you to turn back –

GM: And well they might! The bar is a trap, and if characters do not search they will activate this as they lift the bar. A massive block of stone falls from the ceiling (SPEED 12 to dodge). A character who fails to evade this will be crushed to a pulp.

For those that survive the falling slab:

Beyond the door all is pitch black.
Lantern light seems absorbed by the slick blackness of the walls.
Will you go on. . .?

If they do:

A short corridor brings you to a steep newel staircase that winds up inexorably without door or window. The air is stifling, and your footfalls echo in an eerie quiet.

You clamber up and up. Long after you should have reached the surface, you are still climbing the shadowy twisting newel.

GM: There is no turning back now. Magic has transported them within the black obelisk – Karvala's Tower. Their destiny is to meet a demi-god.

VI. Karvala's Tower

Your legs ache with the climb, and your breaths come in tortured gasps. Reaching the last of your strength, you push through a wall of darkness that seems as thick as swamp mud. Suddenly you are in a clear circular room. Moonlight streams in through wide windows. You feel disorientated; you cannot be sure how long it was since you walked through the ossuary and drew open the black door. . .

Ringing the room are twelve chairs whose high carved backs are etched with symbols of the moon in its various phases. A pattern of lines and symbols covers the floor, as if some arcane game is to be played here. Wooden playing pieces that represent men and beasts, cities and forests, occupy seemingly random positions across the pattern.

GM: The chairs will undoubtedly hold a fatal (*possibly* fatal) fascination for the characters, and at least one of them is likely to be seated. Should this be so, the character will appear grey and insubstantial to his companions, as he becomes a participant in the Game of Karvala. He will remain in the chair until his part in the Game is done.

You must divide the player-characters into two groups — those who have sat in the chairs and those who remained standing.

To any seated character(s):

You stare at the patterns and playing-pieces on the floor, but the sense of it eludes you. Glancing up, you find no sign of your companions!

Through a window opposite you can see the snow-shrouded city bathed in moonlight. Your eyes water without reason, and as you blink a gaunt figure seems to shimmer from the silver beams. He steps towards you, a regal man in pale

robes, ghostly grey in the half-light.

"Welcome," he whispers, "to Karvala's Game..."

GM: While, to the eyes of any characters who have not been so rash as to sit:

A change comes over your comrade. An awful grey in the moonlight, he is as insubstantial as a ghost. You back hastily away and cross yourselves. Your comrade pays no attention to you; he stares with rapt attention at the mysterious pattern on the floor, white knuckles grasping the arms of the chair.

You sense a presence behind you. A tall figure in pale robes stands there. Death comes on a pale horse, they say, and this man is as grey and ghast as that dread rider. His face is thin and aristocratic, and framed by the lunar crescent of his cloak's silver collar.

He gestures at the chair. "What will you give to free your friend?"

GM: Karvala will carry on two simultaneous conversations now, and you must keep the two groups of players separate until events have played their course.

The seated character(s) is enmeshed in Karvala's strange Game. He will soon find that the pieces move on the pattern in response to his thoughts, though he has no inkling of what his moves mean. Gradually, as he watches the moves that Karvala makes, he begins to glean fragments of the befuddling rules of play. Throughout all this, Karvala will speak to the character – it is obvious that he expects a protracted game, and is happy to pepper it with urbane conversation. If the character gets the feeling that he could be playing the Game for centuries, he is right! To represent the abstract intellectual struggle, the player rolls 3d12 and must score equal to or less than his *Intelligence*. If he succeeds, he gets to attempt the same roll again –

he is gaining a small advantage in the Game. If he fails the roll, he suffers a setback in the face of Karvala's superior tactics and spends another day playing on before he gets to attempt the 3d12 roll again. If and when he manages to succeed in this difficult roll ten times in succession, he has beaten Karvala and is free to depart.

This, of course, might take years of game-time! But there is another way for the characters to gain their freedom. Those who have not joined the Game can strike a bargain with Karvala. If he accepts, he will release the seated character(s) from the Game and transport all of them to the citadel gates.

What kind of bargain might be struck? There are many — it is up to the players to think of something that tempts Karvala. He is an immortal, the nearly divine shaman-king of the people who once lived here. He cares naught for earthly pleasures — as he will demonstrate by fashioning moonbeams into a stream of gold and precious stones that vanish as they touch the floor. Neither will threats move him, for within his Tower his abilities and powers are almost without limit. However, trapped within his Tower in self-imposed exile from the world, he yearns for new things. If the characters offer some wild new experiience that they can bring to him, he is likely to accept. Whatever bargain is made must be followed to the letter by Karvala and the characters; he will give them each a torc to wear about their necks. These torcs cannot be removed, and in a year and a day will bring the characters back to the Tower to fulfil their agreement.

If your players are not experienced gamers, they may find the role-playing this situation demands to be beyond them. In this case, have Karvala himself propose the bargain: that they go forth and bring to him, within the space of a year and a day, the sword from the tomb of Elvaron the Elf, a mighty sorcerer of ancient times. If they agree, he will give each a torc and then teleport them out of his Tower. If you go on to use the adventures in **Dragon Warriors 3: The Elven Crystals**, they will indeed find that their fate is to journey to Elvaron's tomb!

VII. Returning to the ship

GM: It takes two days to render the *Linden* seaworthy. If the characters have not returned by then, the baron will have no choice but to set sail without

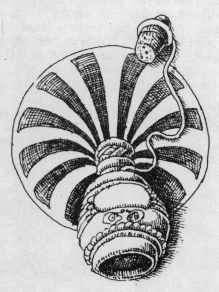

them. He cannot allow anything to jeopardize his mission.

If they return safely, they will be required to hand over any treasure they have found. The baron will then return what he thinks fitting as gifts; these will be items representing half the value of the treasure.

If the characters are wearing Karvala's torcs, they will not of course be able to relinquish these (however much they may wish to!) They will not lose favour for this, because it will be clear to the baron that strange sorcery is at work. However, if the characters are asked about their adventures, they will be unable to speak of the Tower or write down any account of it. Karvala protects his secrets well.

CHARACTER SHEET

Character's Name   **Profession** Mystic **Rank**

Strength =   *Health Points*   ATTACK =
Reflexes =   normal score: DEFENCE =
Intelligence =   current score:
Psychic Talent =   MAGICAL ATTACK =
Looks =   MAGICAL DEFENCE =

                              Psychic Fatigue Check:

Armour   **Equipment**   roll (13 + rank-spell
type worn: level) or less on
Armour Factor: d20 to avoid
                                  psychic fatigue

                              EVASION =

Cash   **Weapons**
Gold Crowns:
Silver Florins:
Copper Pennies:

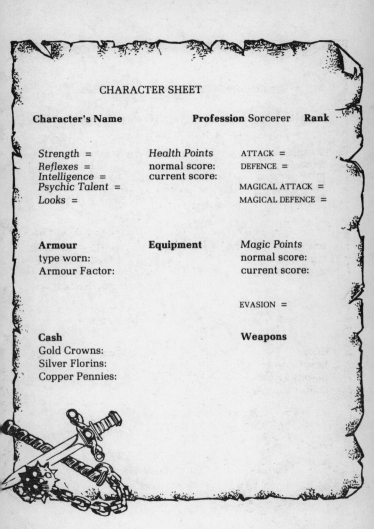

CHARACTER SHEET

Character's Name   **Profession** Sorcerer   **Rank**

Strength =   *Health Points*   ATTACK =
Reflexes =   normal score: DEFENCE =
Intelligence =   current score:
Psychic Talent =   MAGICAL ATTACK =
Looks =   MAGICAL DEFENCE =

Armour   **Equipment**   *Magic Points*
type worn: normal score:
Armour Factor: current score:

                                                       EVASION =

Cash   **Weapons**
Gold Crowns:
Silver Florins:
Copper Pennies:

DRAGON WARRIORS
BOOK ONE
DRAGON WARRIORS

by Dave Morris

The key to a magic world. A land of cobwebbed forests
and haunted castles. A land where dire monsters lurk
in the shadows of the night, where hobgoblins shriek
across the bleak and misty moors, where wizards and
armoured warriors roam dank dungeons in their quest
for gold and glory. The realm of your imagination.

This is the world of DRAGON WARRIORS: a unique
role-playing game in which you and your friends
become the mighty heroes of fantasy.

This first book gives you the essentials for combat, a
complete armoury and a bestiary of bloodthirsty
opponents. You choose the type of warrior you want to
be: an armour-clad Knight, a muscle-bound Barbarian,
a tough Dwarf or a crafty Elf. Take up your sword, your
war axe or your bow. Within ten minutes you will be
battling with your first foe in a perilous adventure.

*Includes one complete scenario: THE KING UNDER
THE FOREST*

DRAGON WARRIORS
THE ULTIMATE ROLE-PLAYING GAME

SBN 0 552 522872

DRAGON WARRIORS
BOOK THREE
THE ELVEN CRYSTALS

by Oliver Johnson

Battle through a monster-filled forest to a lonely well.
Scale the ice-covered towers of a mountain fortress.
Fight with hideous bat-winged foes. Struggle in the
raging surf of a wreck bound reef. Grapple with
horrors from the depths of the sea. Finally you will
reach your goal, deep in a cavern beneath a haunted
island; there an evil priest holds the final fragment of a
thousand year old secret:

What is the mystery behind the Elven Crystals?

This third book of the DRAGON WARRIORS role-
playing game presents *three adventure scenarios* along
with new monsters, magic and treasure which extend
the basic rules of the series. These adventures will take
you and your friends to the limits of your skill and
endurance.

DRAGON WARRIORS
THE ULTIMATE ROLE-PLAYING GAME

SBN 0 552 522899

SAGARD

A NEW SOLO ADVENTURE SERIES FROM THE LEGENDARY CO-CREATOR OF DUNGEONS AND DRAGONS™

by Gary Gygax and Flint Dille

SAGARD 1: THE ICE DRAGON

You are Sagard – a young Barbarian battling the seen and unseen terrors of the Northern Wilderness. In accordance with an age-old tribal custom, you must face the 'Ordeal of Courage' to become a fully-fledged warrior! You will encounter the deadliest of enemies; the razor-clawed Devil Bear and the hideous Great Furred Serpent. But the supreme test of your courage will be to survive the lair of the Ice Dragon!

SBN 0 552 523186

SAGARD 2: THE GREEN HYDRA

You are Sagard – the Barbarian – the lone survivor of a bloody ambush. You must carry out a life-or-death mission for your homeland and tribe and you will encounter unimaginable horrors in this quest: the indestructible Smoke Demon, the hideous Nightripper and the Slith assassin. But will you survive the most dangerous adventure of your life in the Tomb of the Green Hydra?

SBN 0 552 523194

Further titles to come ......

TUNNELS & TROLLS

THE ORIGINAL SOLO ADVENTURE

Have you ever dreamed of being a bold and fearless adventurer? A warrior-king or a wise magician? You can play the part of any of these when you play *Tunnels and Trolls* – the worlds you explore and quests you pursue are limited only by your imagination!

Developed in the USA ten years ago, it is now America's premier solo-playing system, offering a complexity and variety of adventures that far outstrips any of *Tunnels and Trolls'* rivals on the UK market. But *Tunnels and Trolls* is not only a solo role-playing series, although many of its readers were first introduced to it through the twenty solo adventures available: it is a complete role-playing system at a highly competitive price, is both simple to understand and put into action.

Lose yourself for hours in the *Tunnels and Trolls* world . . . .

Five titles now available in the UK in Corgi editions!

TUNNELS & TROLLS

THE TUNNELS AND TROLLS RULE BOOK

The Complete Fantasy Game

All you need to play the Tunnels and Trolls complete fantasy role-playing game! As a Games Master, you direct your friends through the deadly labyrinths that you have designed for their entertainment: this book gives you the framework of how to create complete fantasy characters, use combat and magic with simulated dice rolls – you will be the master of all their actions!

The *complete* Tunnels and Trolls rules for multi-use adventures.

SBN 0 552 127647

TUNNELS AND TROLLS: THE CITY OF TERRORS

Terror has a name: the City of Gull where you will come face-to-face with a thousand Orcs in the city sewers, where you will meet Cronus the Steward of Time in his marbled hall, where you will grip the deadly vampire sword and do battle with the taloned Stalker, where you will arm wrestle in the Black Dragon Tavern over scorpions, where you will barter with Marek the Master Rogue: The City of Terrors, *where just walking in the streets is an adventure!*

SBN 0 552 12768X

TUNNELS & TROLLS

THE ORIGINAL SOLO ADVENTURE

TWO-IN-ONE ADVENTURE GAMEBOOKS WITH COMPLETE EASY-TO-PLAY RULE SYSTEM

NAKED DOOM and DEATHTRAP EQUALIZER

NAKED DOOM: Although innocent, the court have condemned you to the catacombs beneath the city . . . . a fate to which many would have preferred death at the executioner's hand! Will you fall prey to the terrifying monsters that lurk below – or will you be able to make your way back to the light of day and freedom?

DEATHTRAP EQUALIZER: Designed by a death-dealing madman in the City of Kosht, the Deathtrap Equalizer is reached through a teleport gate that will plunge you into a hundred different adventures! Are you clever enough to survive your trip?

SBN 0 552 127671

THE AMULET OF THE SALKTI and ARENA OF KHAZAN

THE AMULET OF THE SALKTI: Deep beneath your home town of Freegore, cloaked in perpetual darkness, past bloody and merciless guardians, lies the Amulet of the Salkti, the only talisman that will avert the evil of the risen demon, Sxelba the Slayer! Will you be able to find it before Sxelba lays all to waste?

ARENA OF KHAZAN: Khazan, City of Death, where the dark sands of the arena are saturated with the blood of slick swordsmen and crafty magicians, where men are forced to battle inhuman hordes of Orcs, Trolls, Dwarves and Ogres under the cold eyes of Khazan's merciless ruler, Khara Khang. Will you survive to win fame and fortune where others have perished?

SBN 0 552 127655

TUNNELS & TROLLS

THE ORIGINAL SOLO ADVENTURE

TWO-IN-ONE ADVENTURE GAMEBOOKS WITH COMPLETE EASY-TO-PLAY RULE SYSTEM

CAPTIF D'YVOIRE and BEYOND THE SILVERED PANE

CAPTIF D'YVOIRE: Taken by surprise, you have been chained up and left to rot in a filthy cell deep in the castle d'Yvoire – you have only your wits with which to escape your sinister jailers! You will need to battle past the guards to face the Dark Forces rallied by the evil Duke. Fight them or remain forever in the dank dungeons of the castle!

BEYOND THE SILVERED PANE: Step through the enchanted Mirror of Marcelanius and enter a world ruled by magic and strife! Barter or battle with dragons, living statues, bandits and behemoths – will you fulfill your quest or be vanquished by your foes?

SBN 0 552 127663

THE BELGARIAD

DAVID EDDINGS

David Eddings has created a wholly imaginary world
whose fate hangs on the outcome of a prophecy made
seven thousand years earlier. The fulfilment of this
prophecy is entrusted to a young farm boy named
Garion, aided by his aunt Pol and the mysterious Mr
Wolf. Together they embark on their quest to retrieve
the stolen Orb of Aldur and confront the ageless malice
of the god Torak.

The story of their quest unfolds with a magical blend of
excitement and enchantment. *The Belgariad* is an out-
standing piece of imaginative storytelling, destined to
achieve the classic status and following of Tolkein's
The Hobbit or Stephen Donaldson's *Chronicles of
Thomas Covenant*.

Pawn of Prophecy	0 552 12284 X	£1.95
Queen of Sorcery	0 552 12348 X	£1.95
Magician's Gambit	0 552 12382 X	£1.95
Castle of Wizardry	0 552 12435 4	£1.95
Enchanters' End Game	0 552 12447 8	£1.95

THE WHITE HART
by Nancy Springer

First in the *Book of Isle* trilogy.

'Three cheers! and a loud Huzzah! for a genuinely *new* fantasy writer'
Anne McCaffrey

Long ago, so long ago that the enchantment of the Beginning was yet on it, there was a little land called Isle. It might have been the entire world for all the people knew; vast oceans encircled the Forest; on the Wastes or the Wealds or the mountain marches of the sea, the Old Ones yet walked; and gods, ghosts and all delvers in the hollow hills were no strangers to the woven shade just beyond the castle gates. It was in those times that *The Book of Suns* got its start, though the Sun Kings knew it only dimly; and a far-flung fate got its start when a lady fair as sunlight loved the Moon King at Laureroc.

0 552 12403 6   £1.75

The second and third titles in this trilogy are also available:

0 552 12426 5   **THE SILVER SUN**
0 552 12427 3   **THE SABLE MOON**

THE DRAGON WAITING
by John M. Ford

'I read it with delight, wonder and fascination. This book plays, with a truly wonderful seriousness, the game of fantasy and history. I love it'
Marion Zimmer Bradley, author of *The Mists of Avalon*

Across Europe, forces of darkness, magic and rebellion are gathering, bringing the Vampire Duke of Milan, an exiled heir to the Byzantine throne and a young woman physician closer to confrontations that will involve Richard, Duke of Gloucester, Louis VI of France and a plotting wizard spy. And meanwhile, in the Welsh hills, Hywell Peredur watches the Red Dragon rise again to free his country from the White Dragon of England. And the Dragon is waiting for each of them . . .

The Dragon Waiting is a fantasy of stupendous scope and richness, a glittering tapestry of passion and betrayal, magic and intrigue, a magnificent recreation of a past where myth has become history.

'A thunderclap of a book, a thing of blood and magic'
Roger Zelazny

0 552 12557 1

£3.50